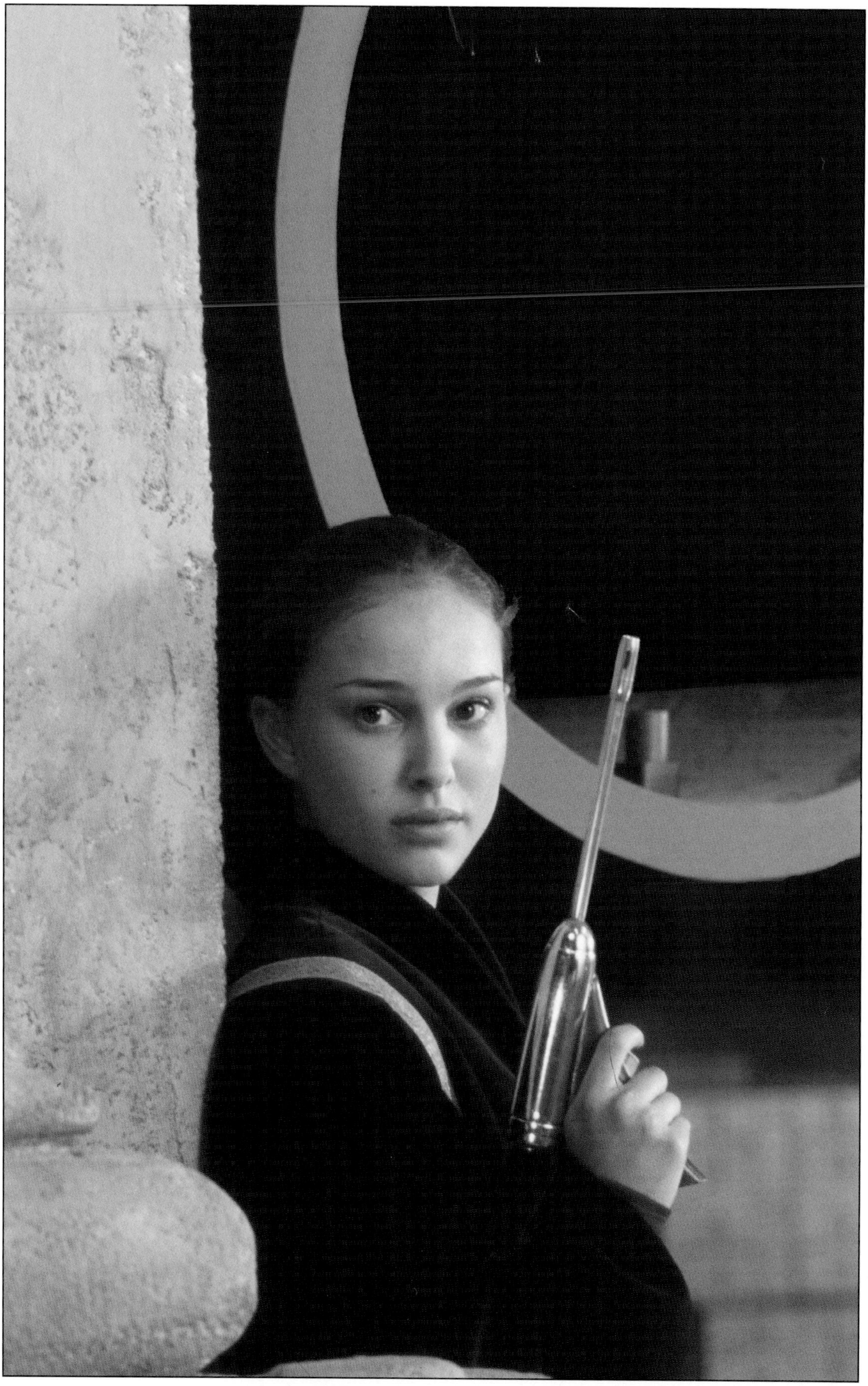

STAR WARS®

EPISODE I
THE PHANTOM MENACE™

VOLUME FOUR

ADAPTED BY
HENRY GILROY

FROM AN ORIGINAL STORY BY
GEORGE LUCAS

PENCILS
RODOLFO DAMAGGIO

INKS
AL WILLIAMSON

COLORS
DAVE NESTELLE

COLOR SEPARATOR
HAROLD MACKINNON

LETTERS
STEVE DUTRO

COVER ART
HUGH FLEMING

DARK HORSE COMICS

Spotlight

VISIT US AT
www.abdopublishing.com

Reinforced library bound edition published in 2009 by Spotlight, a division of the ABDO Group, 8000 West 78th Street, Edina, Minnesota 55439. Spotlight produces high-quality reinforced library bound editions for schools and libraries. Published by agreement with Dark Horse Comics, Inc., and Lucasfilm Ltd.

Library of Congress Cataloging-in-Publication Data

Gilroy, Henry.
Episode I : the phantom menace / story, George Lucas ; script, Henry Gilroy ; pencils, Rodolfo Damaggio ; inks, Al Williamson ; colors, Dave Nestelle ; letters, Steve Dutro. -- Reinforced library bound ed.
p. cm. -- (Star Wars)
ISBN 978-1-59961-608-7 (v.1) -- ISBN 978-1-59961-609-4 (v.2) -- ISBN 978-1-59961-610-0 (v.3) -- ISBN 978-1-59961-611-7 (v.4)
1. Graphic novels. [1. Graphic novels.] I. Lucas, George, 1944- II. Damaggio, Rodolfo. III. Williamson, Al, 1931- IV. Nestelle, Dave. V. Dutro, Steve. VI. Star wars, episode I, the phantom menace (Motion picture) VII. Title.
PZ7.7.G55Epi 2009
[Fic]--dc22

2008038310

Spotlight

All Spotlight books have reinforced library bindings and are manufactured in the United States of America.

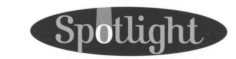

Episode I

THE PHANTOM MENACE

Volume 4

Anakin Skywalker's Podrace victory has
not only enabled Queen Amidala's ship to
be repaired, it has also freed him to go with
Qui-Gon Jinn and Obi-Wan Kenobi to
appeal to the Jedi Council for a chance to
train as a Jedi Knight.

Finally en route to the Senate meeting—
where Amidala will plea for help against
the Trade Federation's invasion of her
planet—the Jedi Knights foil an attempt to
kidnap the Queen, and are thereby alerted
to the possible return of the Sith to the
galaxy.

The Senate and Jedi Council both have
denied the requests set before them,
forcing the Queen to decide in favor of war.
She has returned to her planet, with
Qui-Gon and Obi-Wan for protection, with
the hope of allying with the Gungans
against the Trade Federation . . .

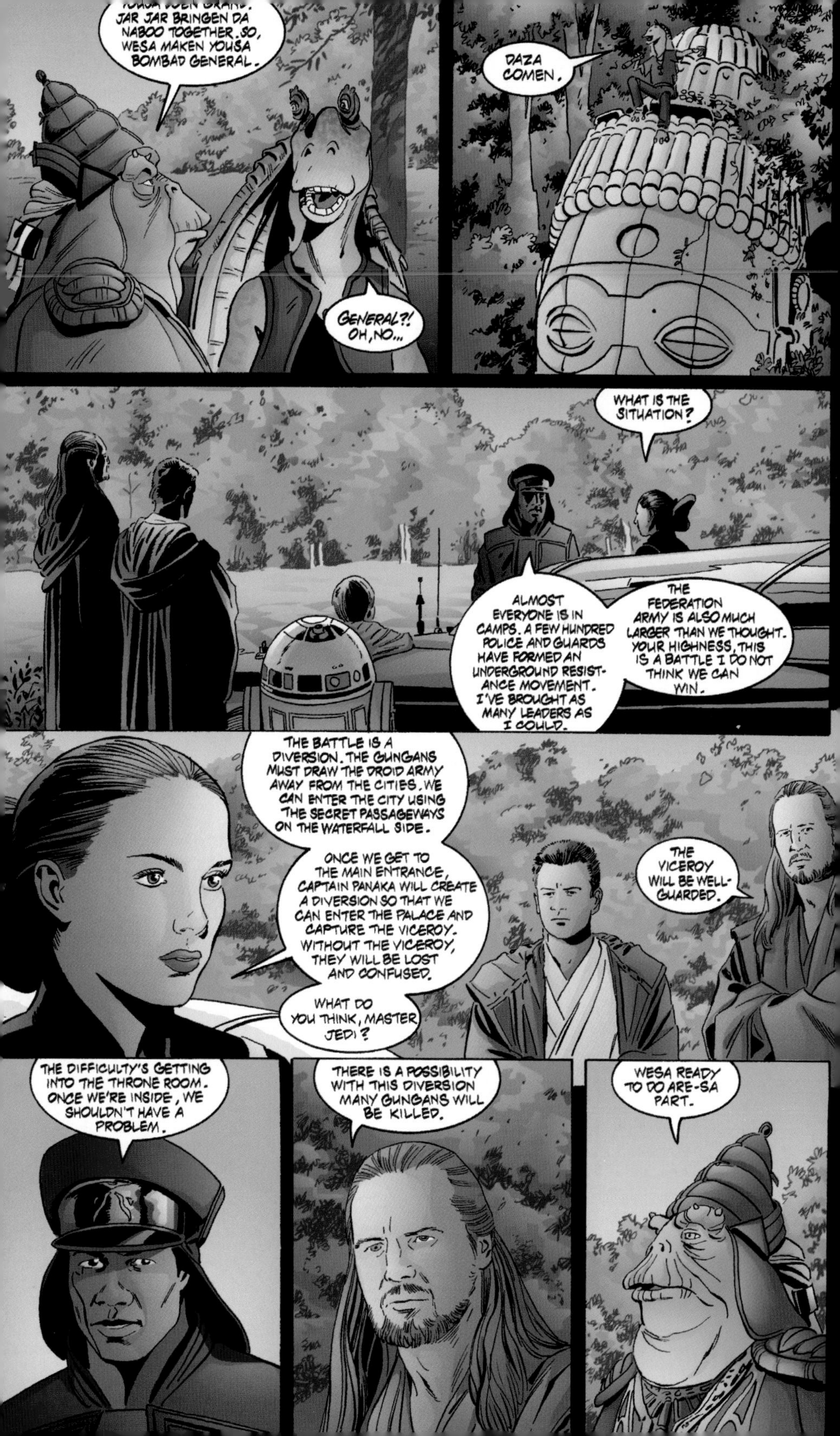
JAR JAR BRINGEN DA NABOO TOGETHER. SO, WESA MAKEN YOUSA BOMBAD GENERAL.
GENERAL?! OH, NO...
DAZA COMEN.
WHAT IS THE SITUATION?
ALMOST EVERYONE IS IN CAMPS. A FEW HUNDRED POLICE AND GUARDS HAVE FORMED AN UNDERGROUND RESISTANCE MOVEMENT. I'VE BROUGHT AS MANY LEADERS AS I COULD.
THE FEDERATION ARMY IS ALSO MUCH LARGER THAN WE THOUGHT. YOUR HIGHNESS, THIS IS A BATTLE I DO NOT THINK WE CAN WIN.
THE BATTLE IS A DIVERSION. THE GUNGANS MUST DRAW THE DROID ARMY AWAY FROM THE CITIES. WE CAN ENTER THE CITY USING THE SECRET PASSAGEWAYS ON THE WATERFALL SIDE.
ONCE WE GET TO THE MAIN ENTRANCE, CAPTAIN PANAKA WILL CREATE A DIVERSION SO THAT WE CAN ENTER THE PALACE AND CAPTURE THE VICEROY. WITHOUT THE VICEROY, THEY WILL BE LOST AND CONFUSED.
WHAT DO YOU THINK, MASTER JEDI?
THE VICEROY WILL BE WELL-GUARDED.
THE DIFFICULTY'S GETTING INTO THE THRONE ROOM. ONCE WE'RE INSIDE, WE SHOULDN'T HAVE A PROBLEM.
THERE IS A POSSIBILITY WITH THIS DIVERSION MANY GUNGANS WILL BE KILLED.
WESA READY TO DO ARE-SA PART.

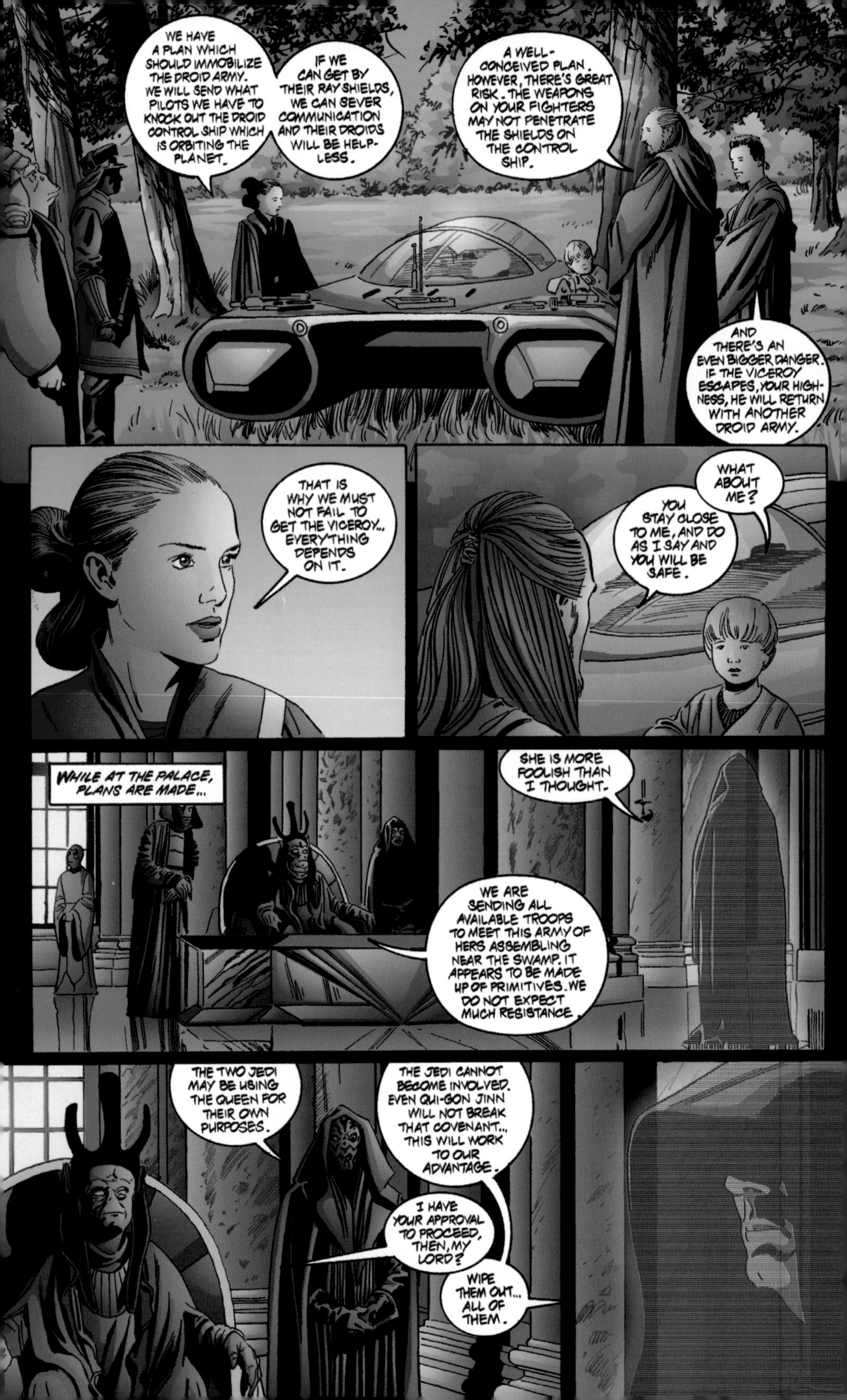
WE HAVE A PLAN WHICH SHOULD IMMOBILIZE THE DROID ARMY. WE WILL SEND WHAT PILOTS WE HAVE TO KNOCK OUT THE DROID CONTROL SHIP WHICH IS ORBITING THE PLANET.
IF WE CAN GET BY THEIR RAY SHIELDS, WE CAN SEVER COMMUNICATION AND THEIR DROIDS WILL BE HELPLESS.
A WELL-CONCEIVED PLAN. HOWEVER, THERE'S GREAT RISK. THE WEAPONS ON YOUR FIGHTERS MAY NOT PENETRATE THE SHIELDS ON THE CONTROL SHIP.
AND THERE'S AN EVEN BIGGER DANGER. IF THE VICEROY ESCAPES, YOUR HIGHNESS, HE WILL RETURN WITH ANOTHER DROID ARMY.
THAT IS WHY WE MUST NOT FAIL TO GET THE VICEROY... EVERYTHING DEPENDS ON IT.
WHAT ABOUT ME?
YOU STAY CLOSE TO ME, AND DO AS I SAY AND YOU WILL BE SAFE.
WHILE AT THE PALACE, PLANS ARE MADE...
SHE IS MORE FOOLISH THAN I THOUGHT.
WE ARE SENDING ALL AVAILABLE TROOPS TO MEET THIS ARMY OF HERS ASSEMBLING NEAR THE SWAMP. IT APPEARS TO BE MADE UP OF PRIMITIVES. WE DO NOT EXPECT MUCH RESISTANCE.
THE TWO JEDI MAY BE USING THE QUEEN FOR THEIR OWN PURPOSES.
THE JEDI CANNOT BECOME INVOLVED. EVEN QUI-GON JINN WILL NOT BREAK THAT COVENANT... THIS WILL WORK TO OUR ADVANTAGE.
I HAVE YOUR APPROVAL TO PROCEED, THEN, MY LORD?
WIPE THEM OUT... ALL OF THEM.

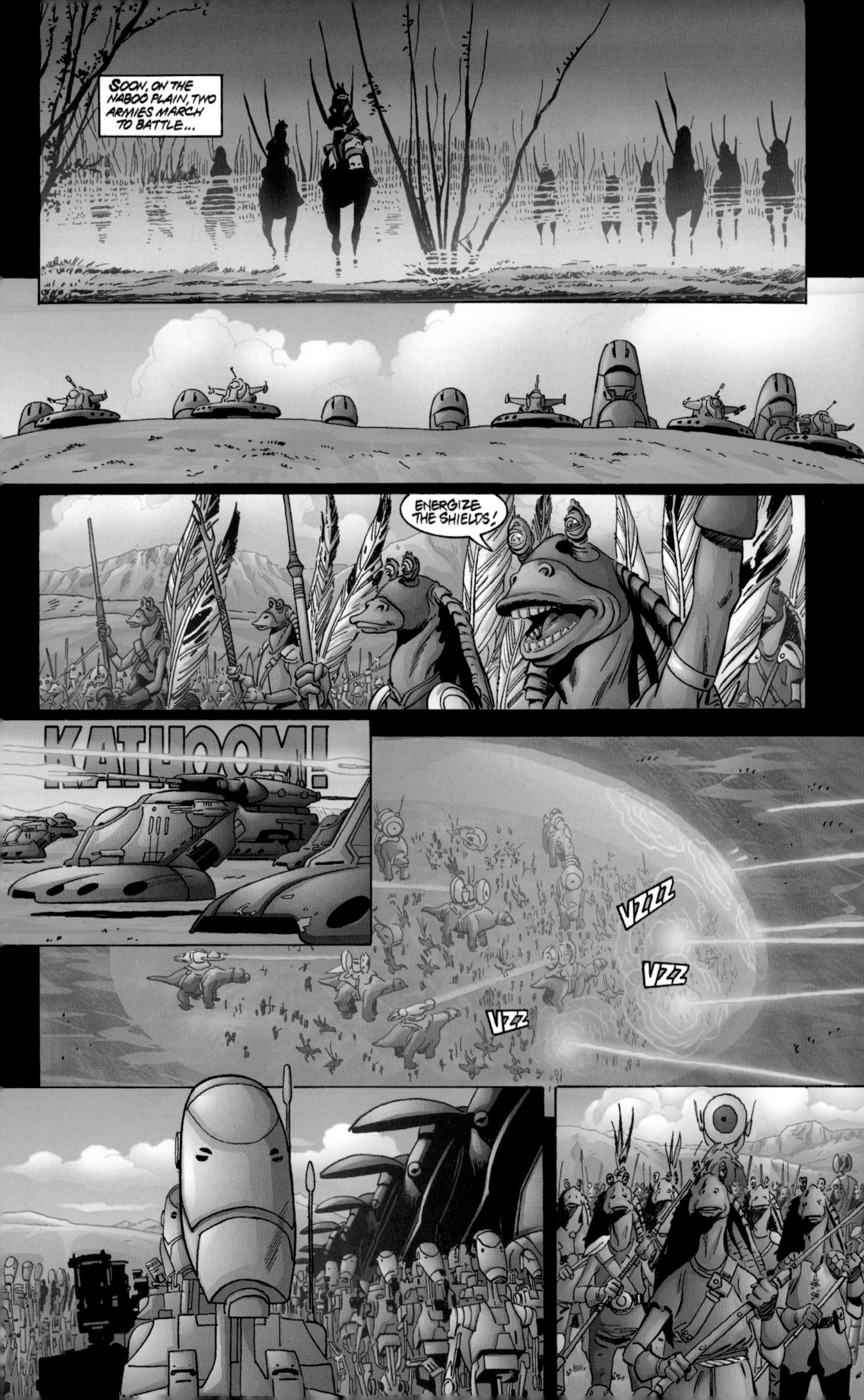
SOON, ON THE NABOO PLAIN, TWO ARMIES MARCH TO BATTLE...
ENERGIZE THE SHIELDS!
KATHOOM!
VZZZZ
VZZ
VZZ

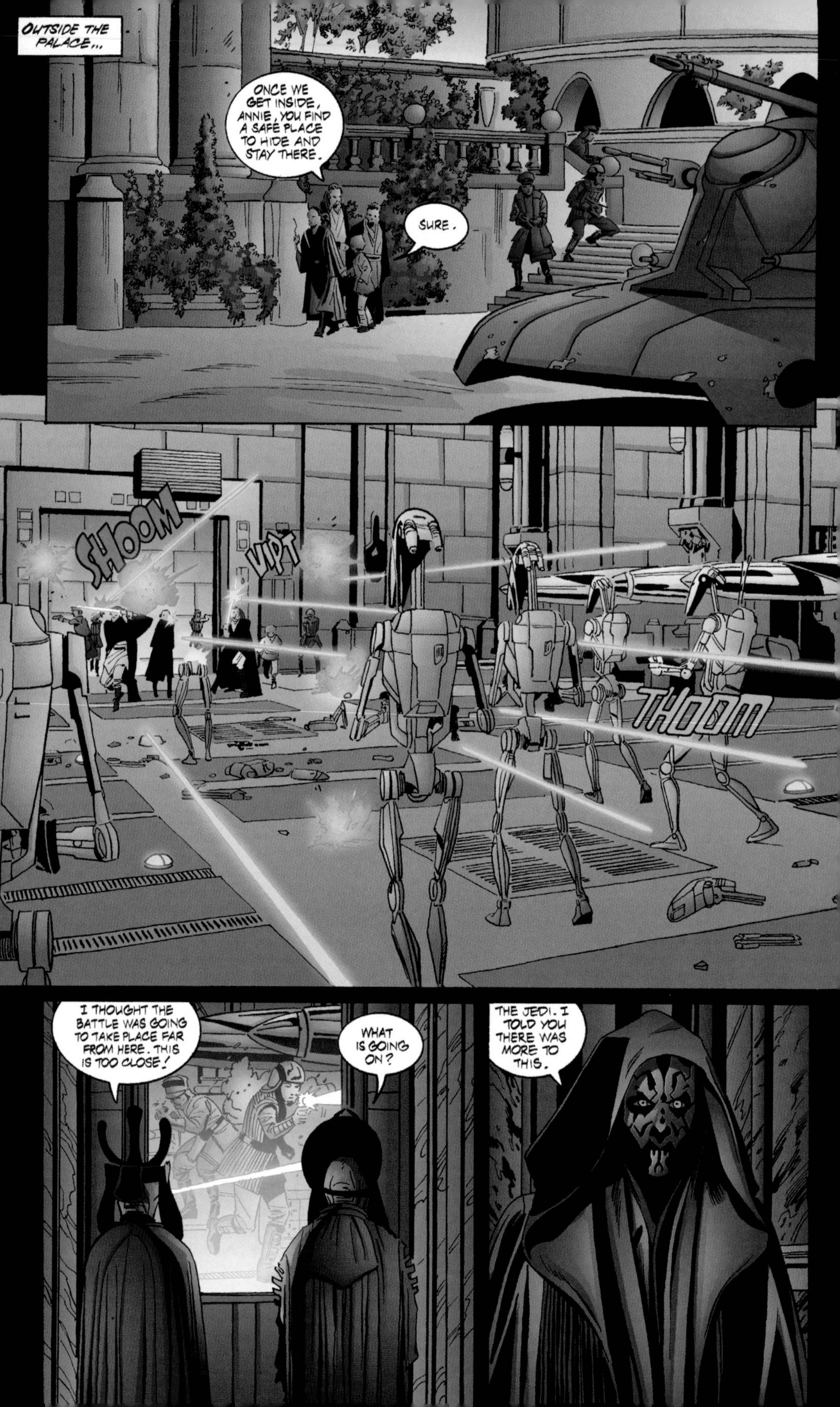
OUTSIDE THE PALACE...
ONCE WE GET INSIDE, ANNIE, YOU FIND A SAFE PLACE TO HIDE AND STAY THERE.
SURE.
SHOOM
VIPT
THOOM
I THOUGHT THE BATTLE WAS GOING TO TAKE PLACE FAR FROM HERE. THIS IS TOO CLOSE!
WHAT IS GOING ON?
THE JEDI. I TOLD YOU THERE WAS MORE TO THIS.

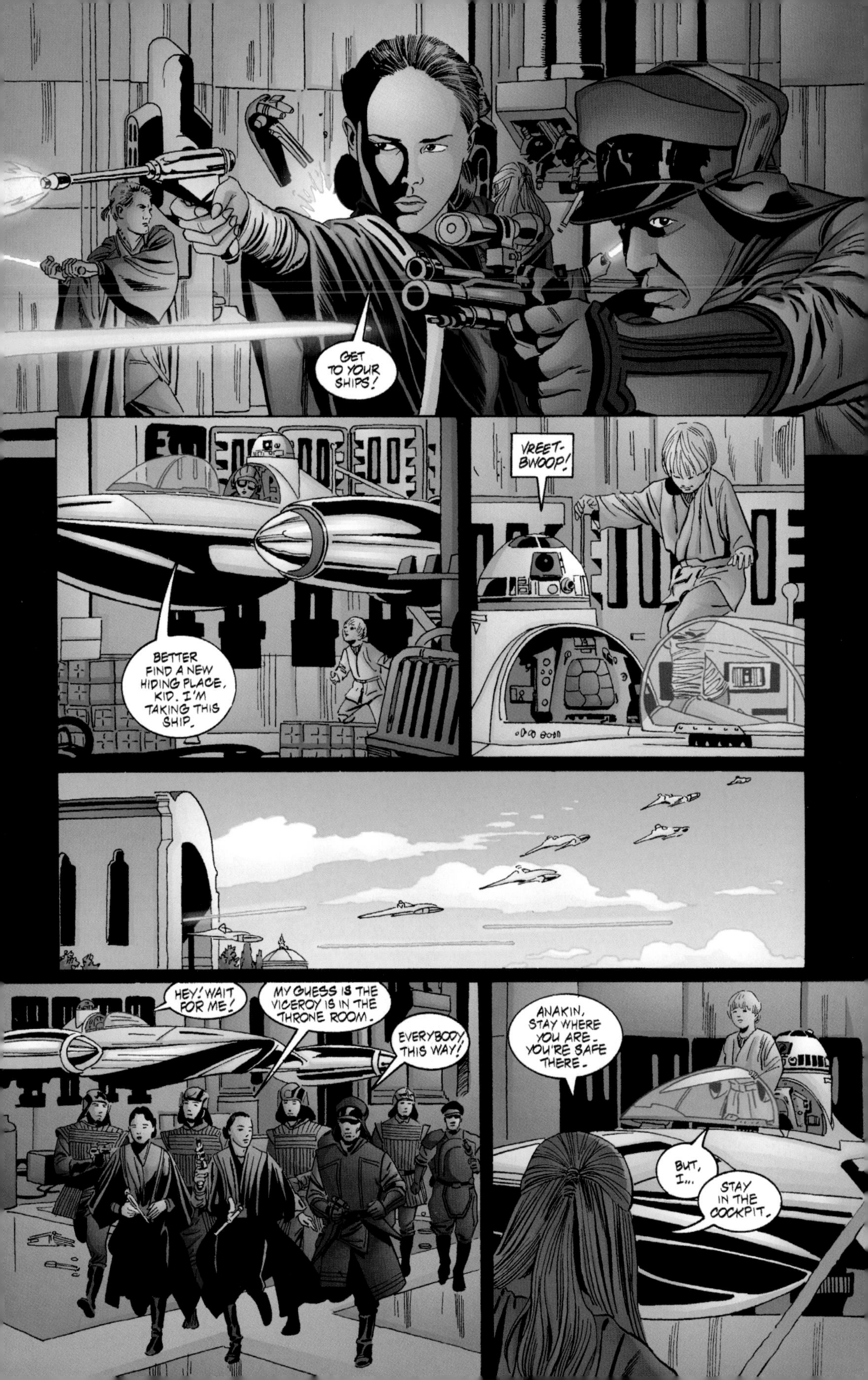
GET TO YOUR SHIPS!
BETTER FIND A NEW HIDING PLACE, KID. I'M TAKING THIS SHIP.
VREET-BWOOP!
HEY! WAIT FOR ME!
MY GUESS IS THE VICEROY IS IN THE THRONE ROOM.
EVERYBODY, THIS WAY!
ANAKIN, STAY WHERE YOU ARE. YOU'RE SAFE THERE.
BUT, I...
STAY IN THE COCKPIT.

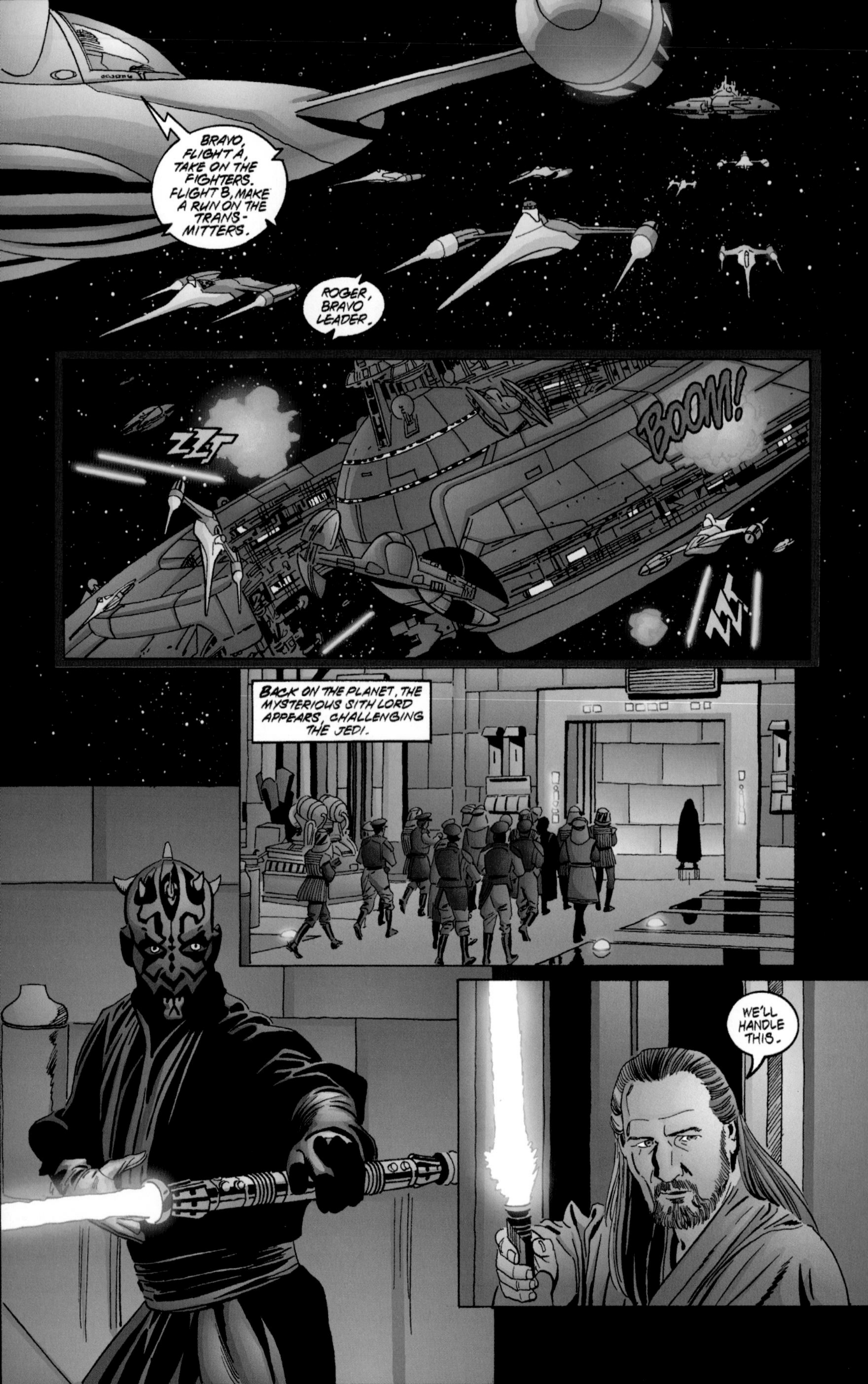
BRAVO, FLIGHT A, TAKE ON THE FIGHTERS. FLIGHT B, MAKE A RUN ON THE TRANS-MITTERS.
ROGER, BRAVO LEADER.
ZZT
BOOM!
ZZT
BACK ON THE PLANET, THE MYSTERIOUS SITH LORD APPEARS, CHALLENGING THE JEDI.
WE'LL HANDLE THIS.

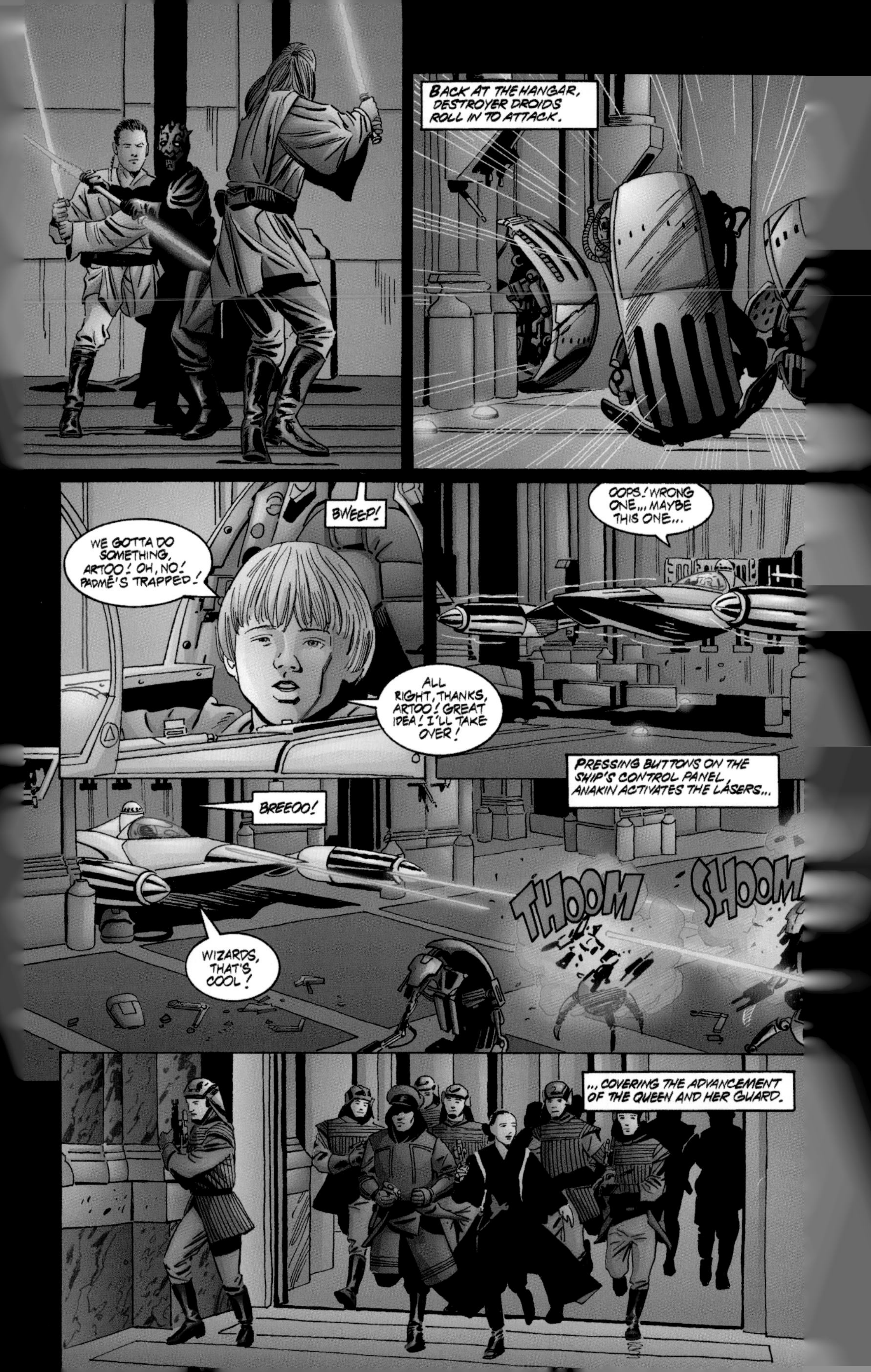
BACK AT THE HANGAR, DESTROYER DROIDS ROLL IN TO ATTACK.
BWEEP!
WE GOTTA DO SOMETHING, ARTOO! OH, NO! PADMÉ'S TRAPPED!
ALL RIGHT, THANKS, ARTOO! GREAT IDEA! I'LL TAKE OVER!
OOPS! WRONG ONE... MAYBE THIS ONE...
PRESSING BUTTONS ON THE SHIP'S CONTROL PANEL, ANAKIN ACTIVATES THE LASERS...
BREEOO!
THOOM
SHOOM
WIZARDS, THAT'S COOL!
...COVERING THE ADVANCEMENT OF THE QUEEN AND HER GUARD.

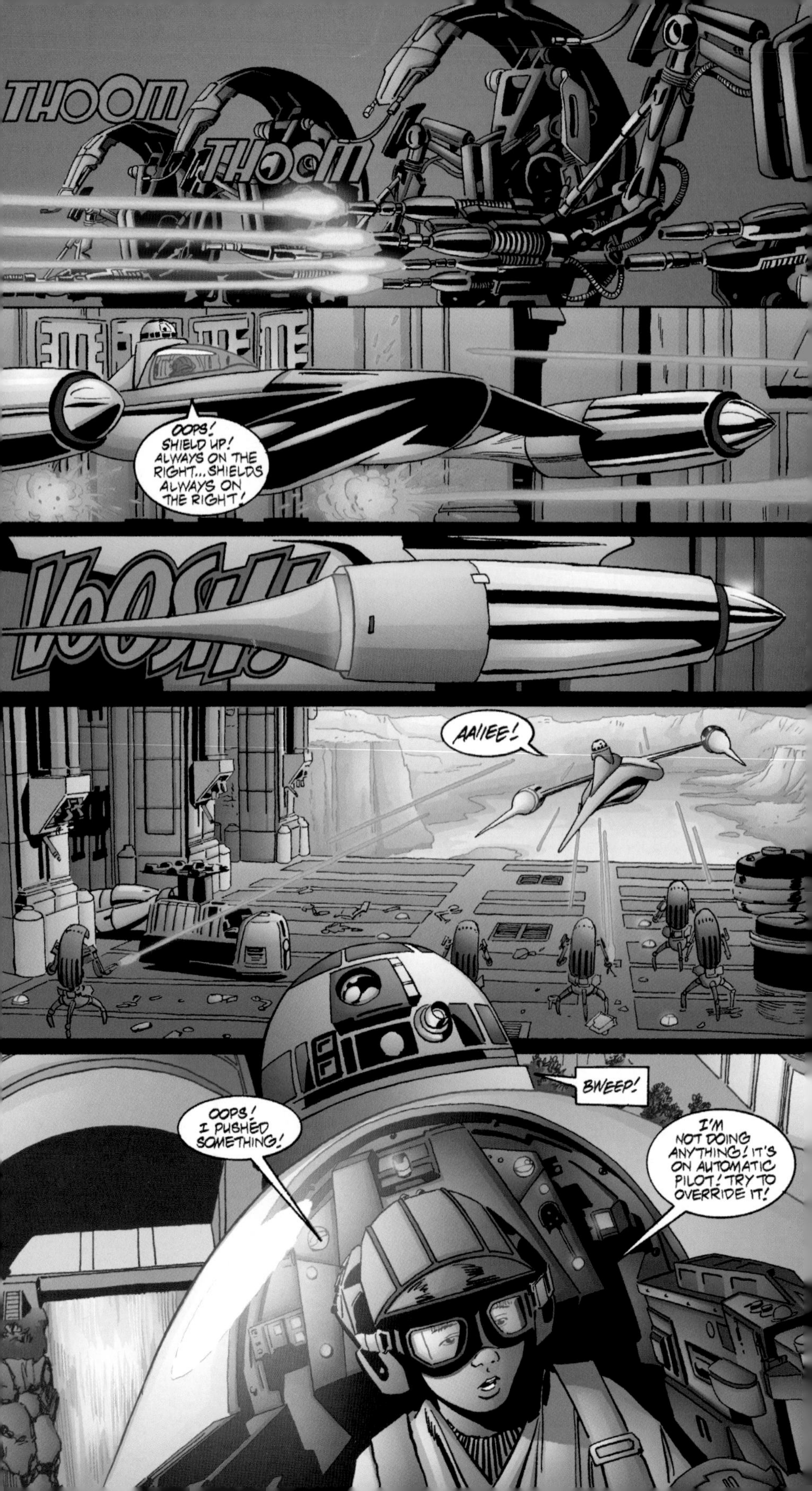
THOOM
THOOM
OOPS! SHIELD UP! ALWAYS ON THE RIGHT... SHIELDS ALWAYS ON THE RIGHT!
VOOSH!
AAIIEE!
BWEEP!
OOPS! I PUSHED SOMETHING!
I'M NOT DOING ANYTHING! IT'S ON AUTOMATIC PILOT! TRY TO OVERRIDE IT!

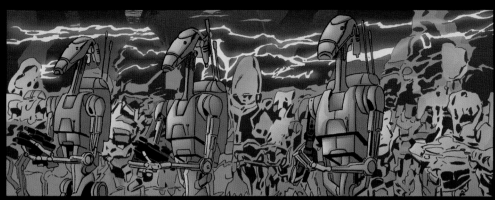

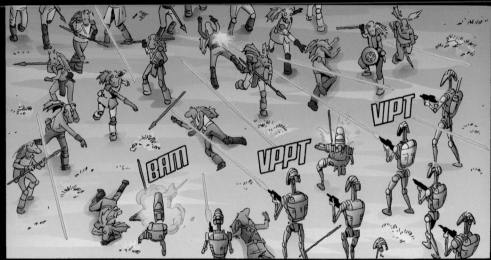

VIPT

BAM

VPPT

WHILE AT THE PALACE...

WE DON'T HAVE TIME FOR THIS, CAPTAIN.

ABOVE NABOO...

WHOO, BOY! THIS IS TENSE! ARTOO, GET US OFF AUTO-PILOT!

BWEEP?

YES, I'VE GOT CONTROL. YOU DID IT, ARTOO!

VREET-DOOP!

GO BACK?! QUI-GON TOLD ME TO STAY IN THIS COCKPIT AND THAT'S WHAT I'M GONNA DO. NOW C'MON!

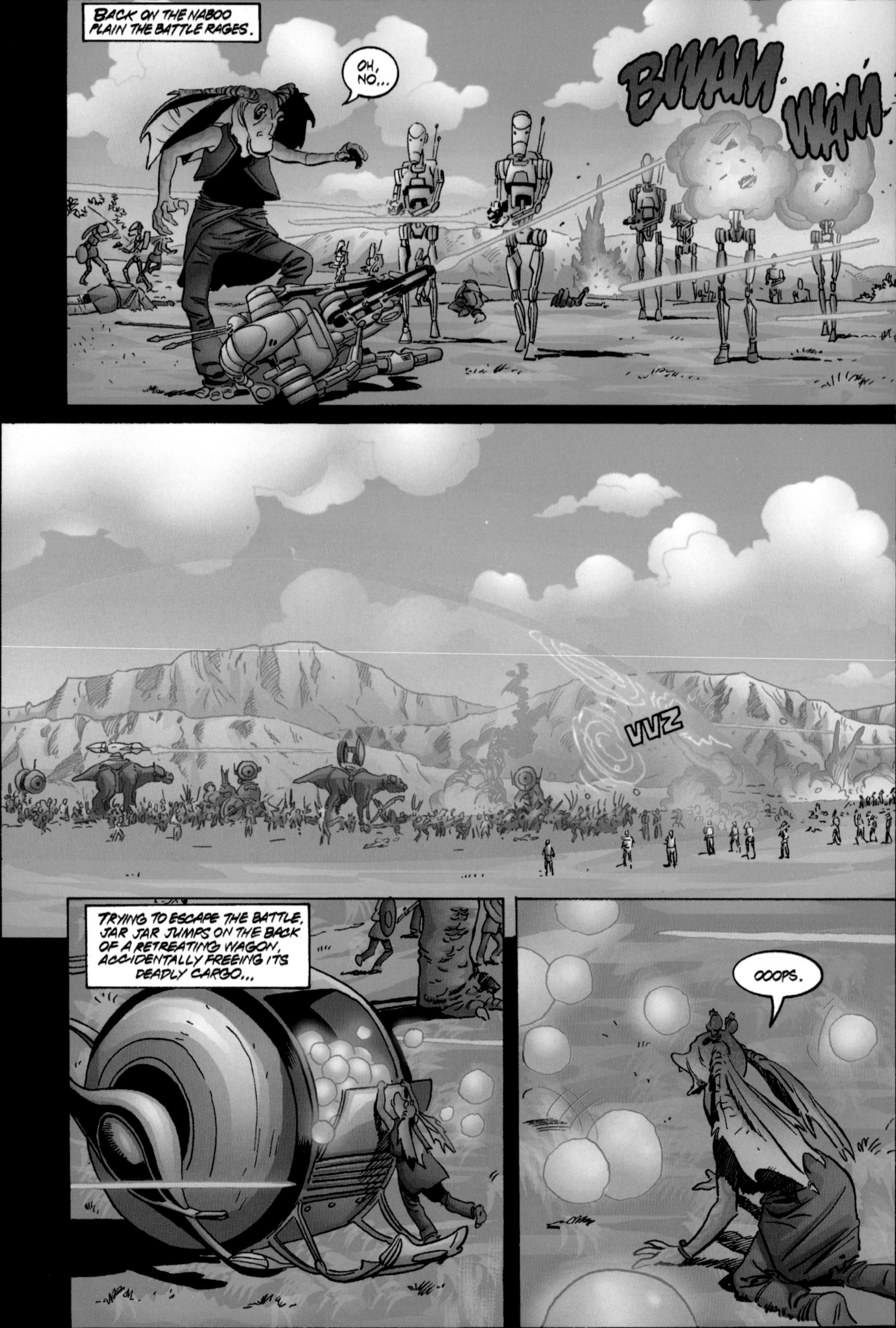
BACK ON THE NABOO PLAIN THE BATTLE RAGES.
OH, NO...
BWAM
WAM
VVZ
TRYING TO ESCAPE THE BATTLE, JAR JAR JUMPS ON THE BACK OF A RETREATING WAGON, ACCIDENTALLY FREEING ITS DEADLY CARGO...
OOOPS.

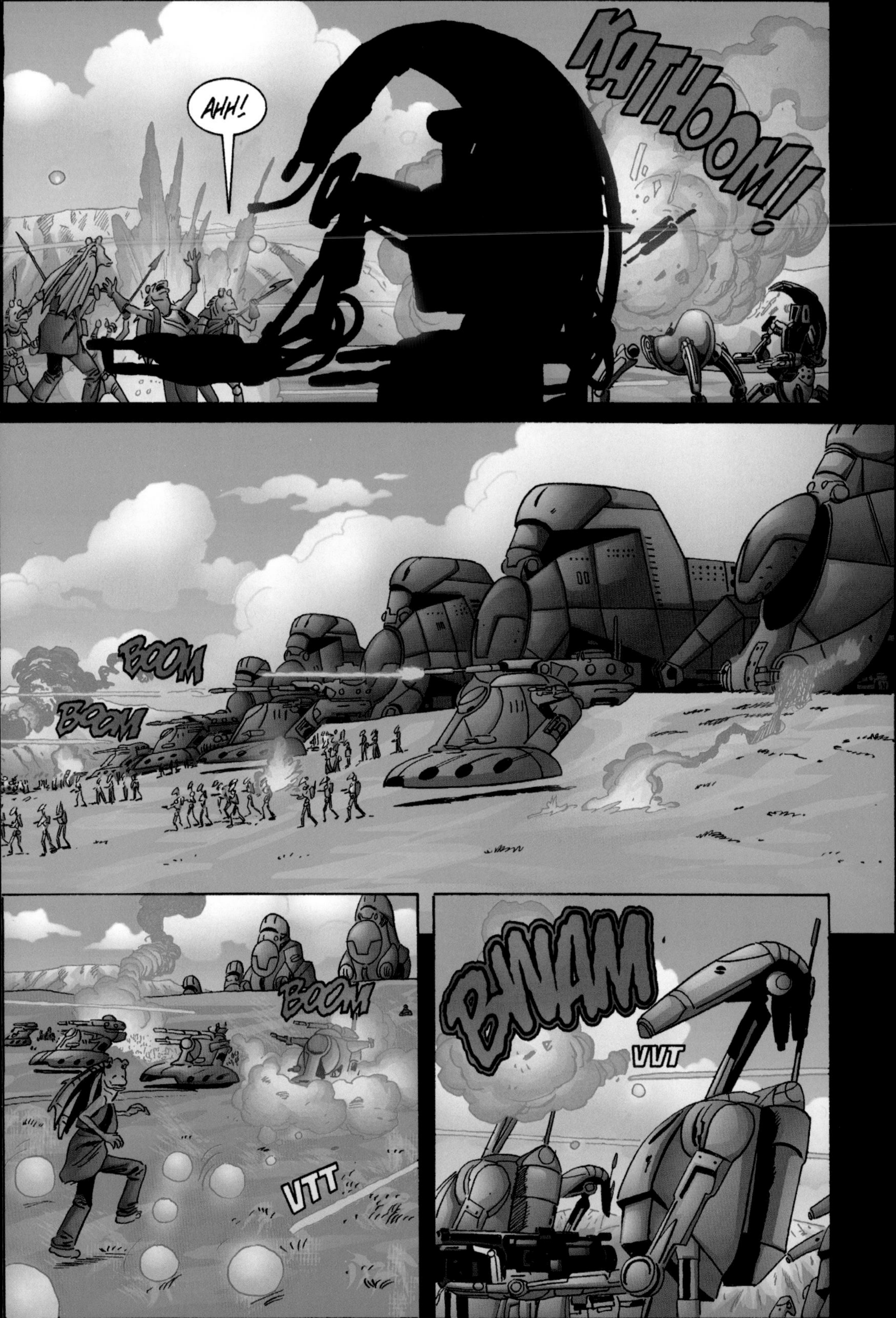
AHH!
KATHOOM!
BOOM
BOOM
BOOM
VTT
BWAM
VVT

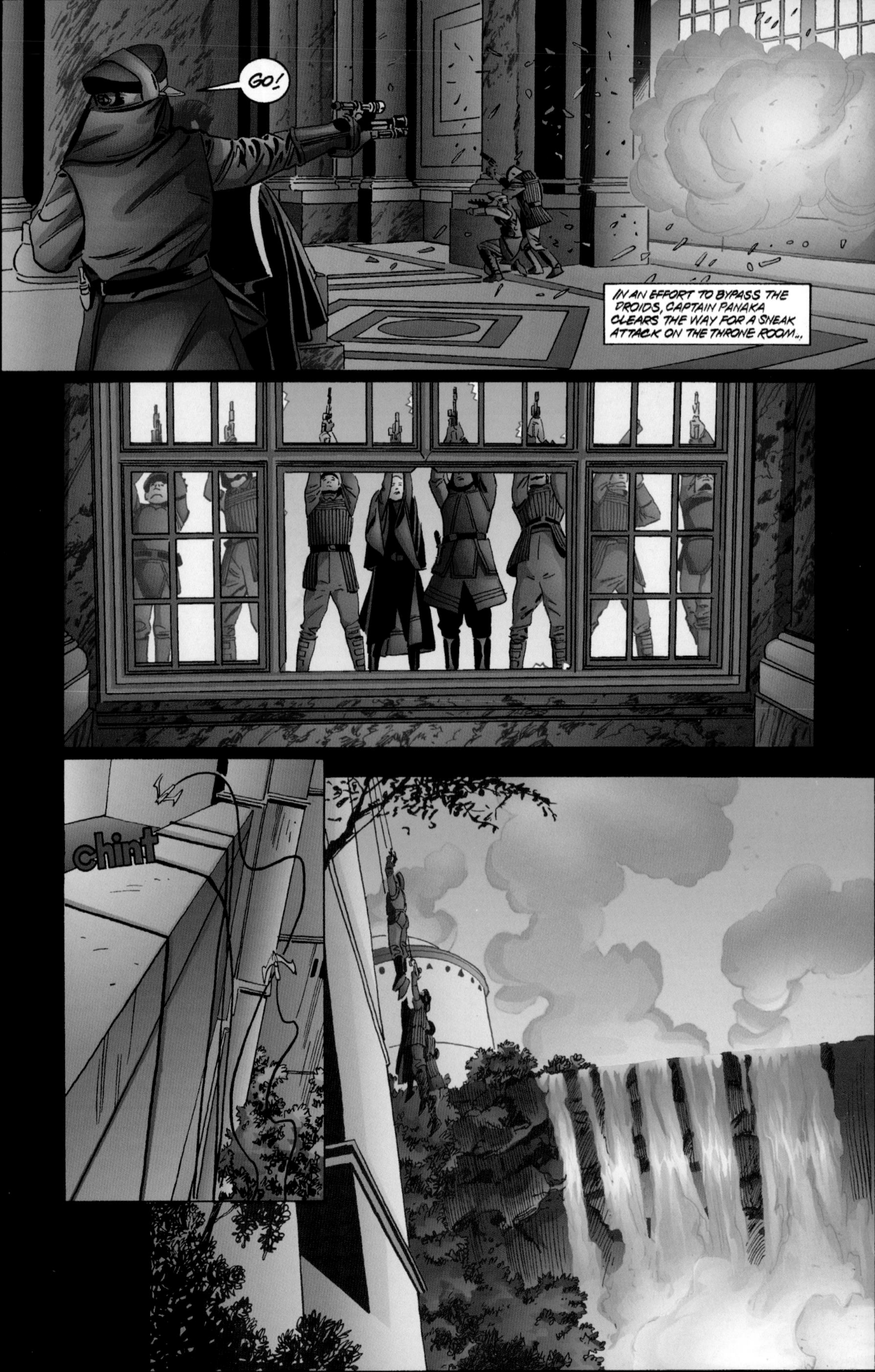
GO!
IN AN EFFORT TO BYPASS THE DROIDS, CAPTAIN PANAKA CLEARS THE WAY FOR A SNEAK ATTACK ON THE THRONE ROOM...
chint

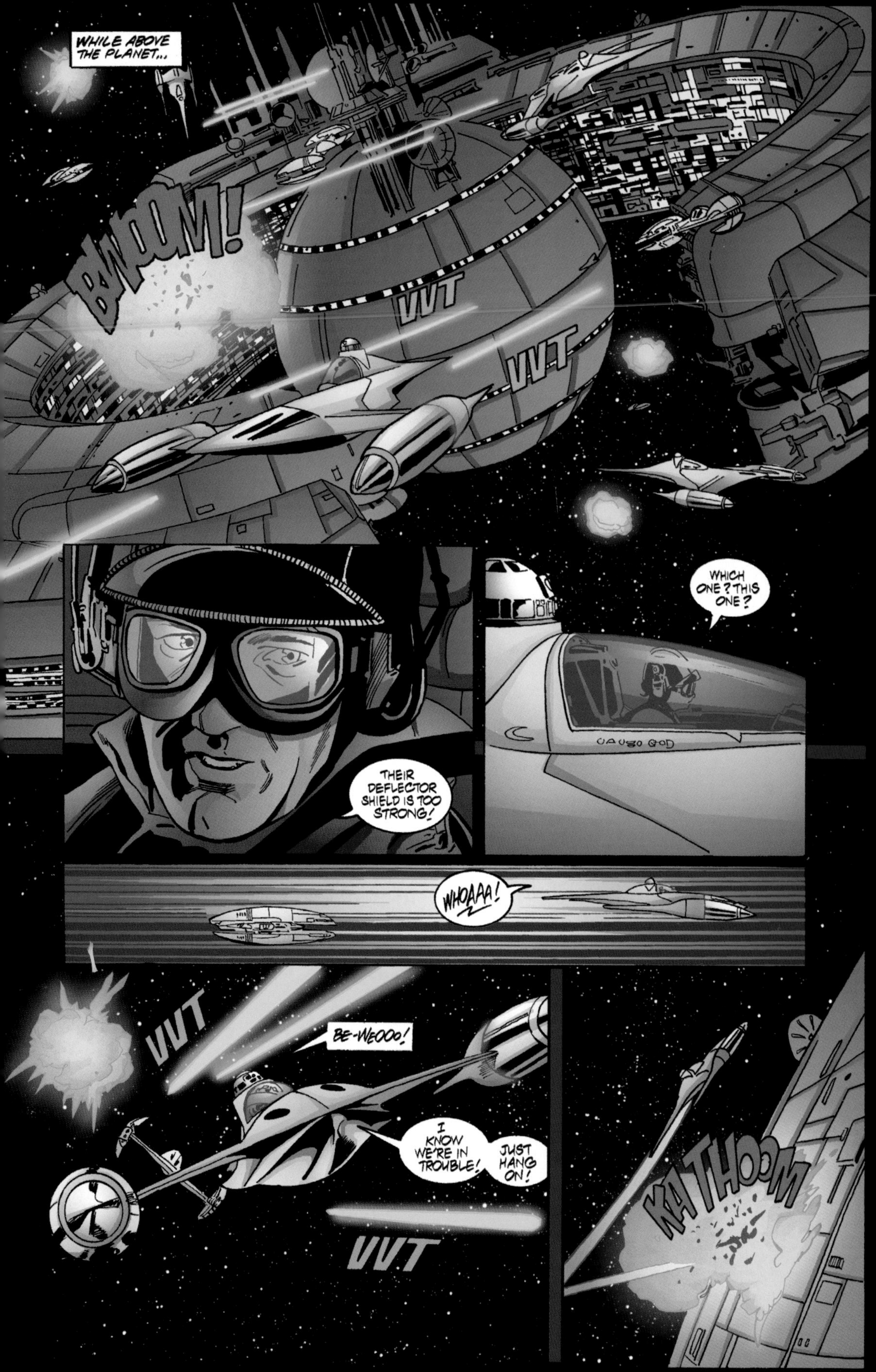

WHILE ABOVE THE PLANET...
BAROOM!
VVT
VVT
THEIR DEFLECTOR SHIELD IS TOO STRONG!
WHICH ONE? THIS ONE?
WHOAAA!
VVT
BE-WEOOO!
I KNOW WE'RE IN TROUBLE!
JUST HANG ON!
VVT
KATHOOM

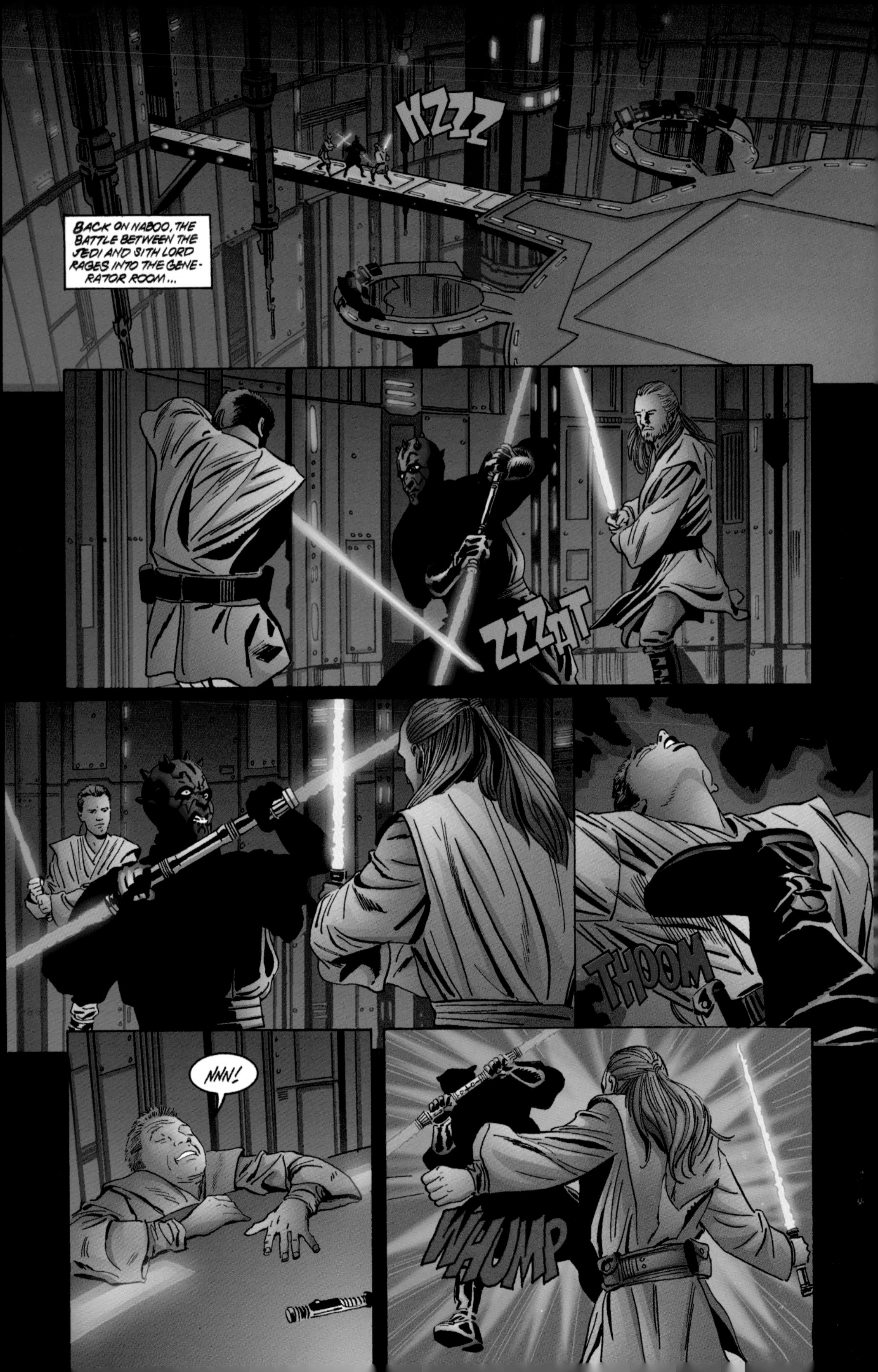
HZZZ
BACK ON NABOO, THE BATTLE BETWEEN THE JEDI AND SITH LORD RAGES INTO THE GENERATOR ROOM...
ZZZAT
THOOM
NNN!
WHUMP

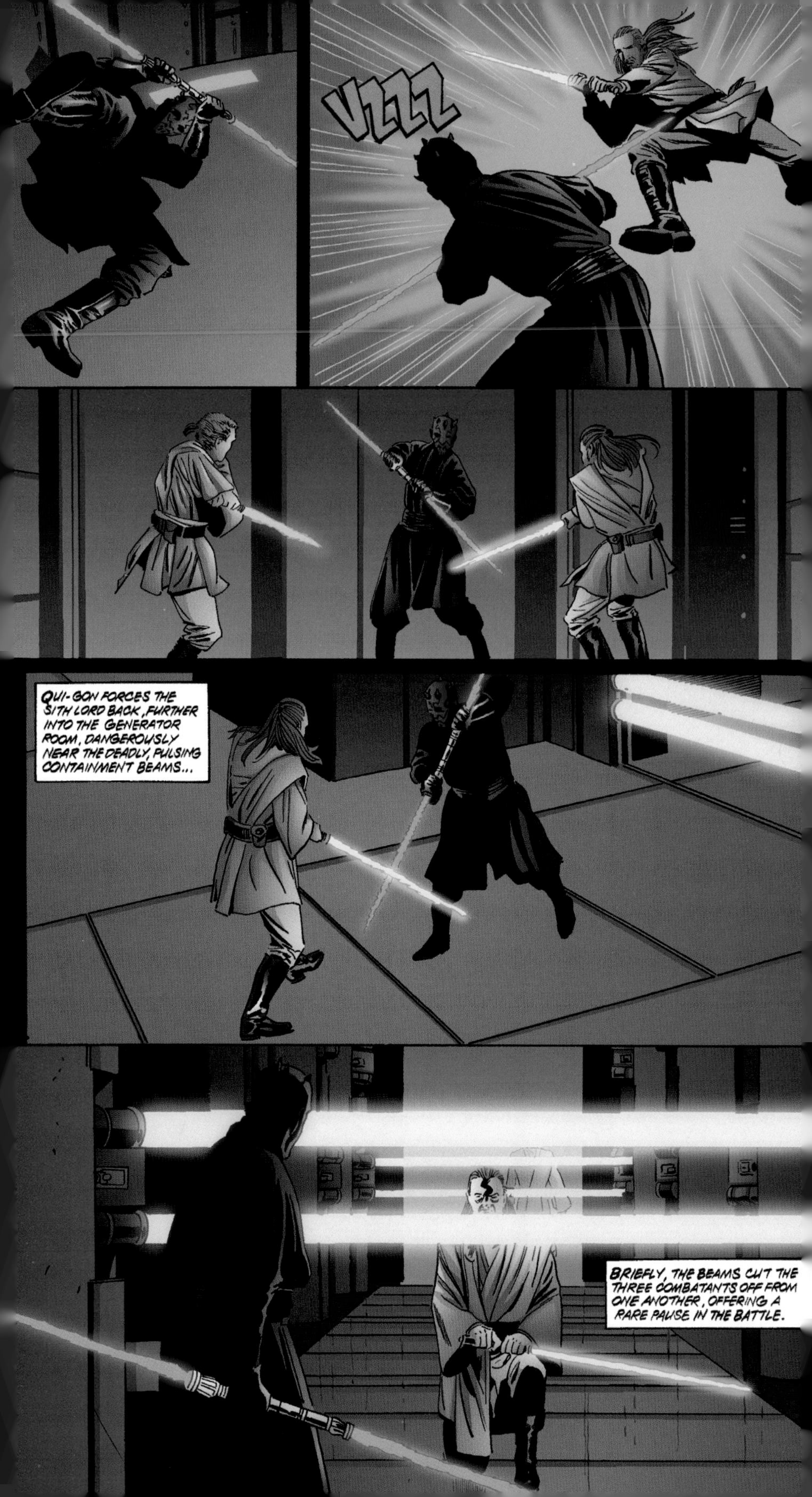
VZZZ
QUI-GON FORCES THE SITH LORD BACK, FURTHER INTO THE GENERATOR ROOM, DANGEROUSLY NEAR THE DEADLY, PULSING CONTAINMENT BEAMS...
BRIEFLY, THE BEAMS CUT THE THREE COMBATANTS OFF FROM ONE ANOTHER, OFFERING A RARE PAUSE IN THE BATTLE.

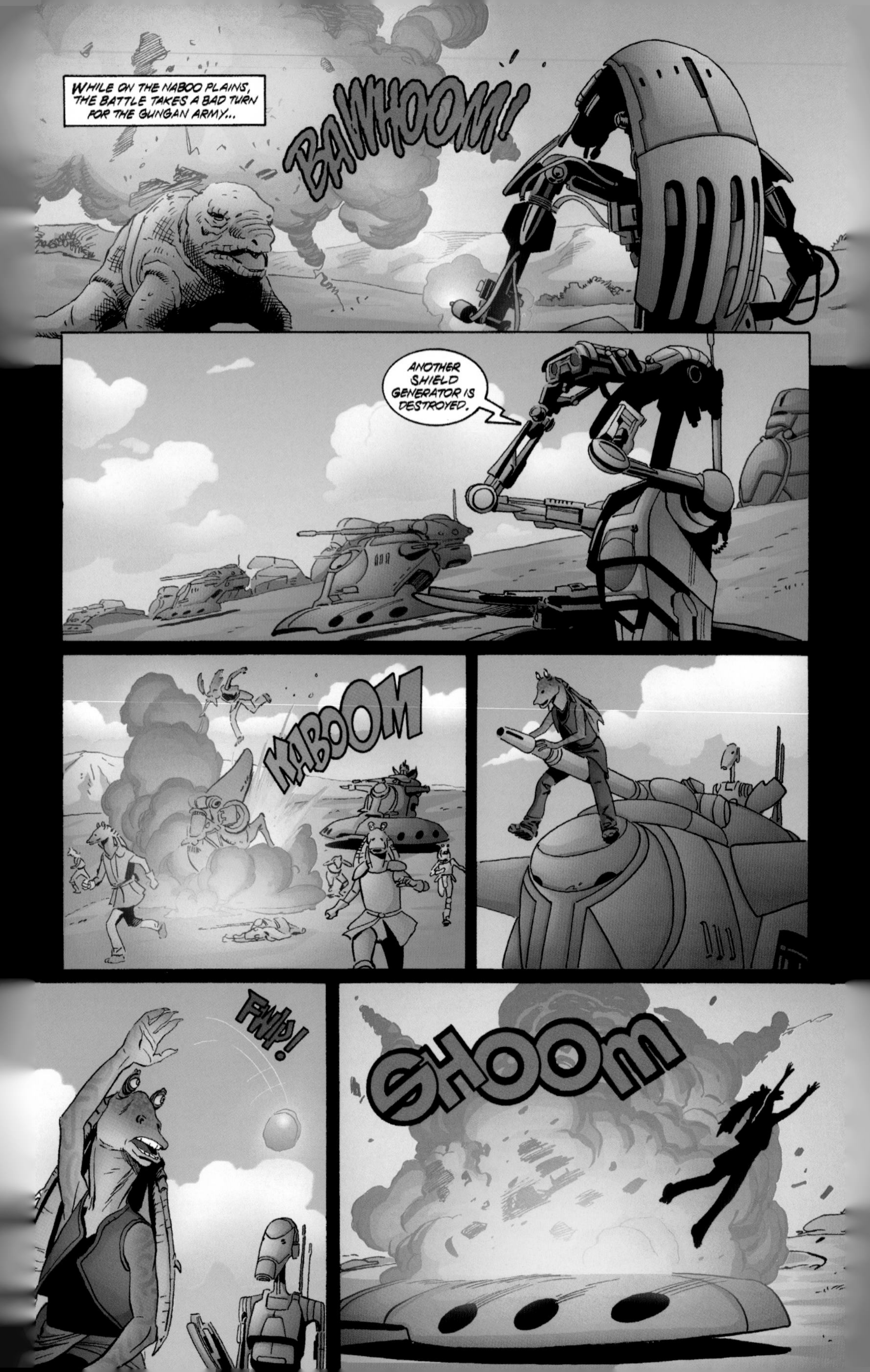
WHILE ON THE NABOO PLAINS, THE BATTLE TAKES A BAD TURN FOR THE GUNGAN ARMY...
BAWHOOM!
ANOTHER SHIELD GENERATOR IS DESTROYED.
KABOOM
FWIP!
SHOOM

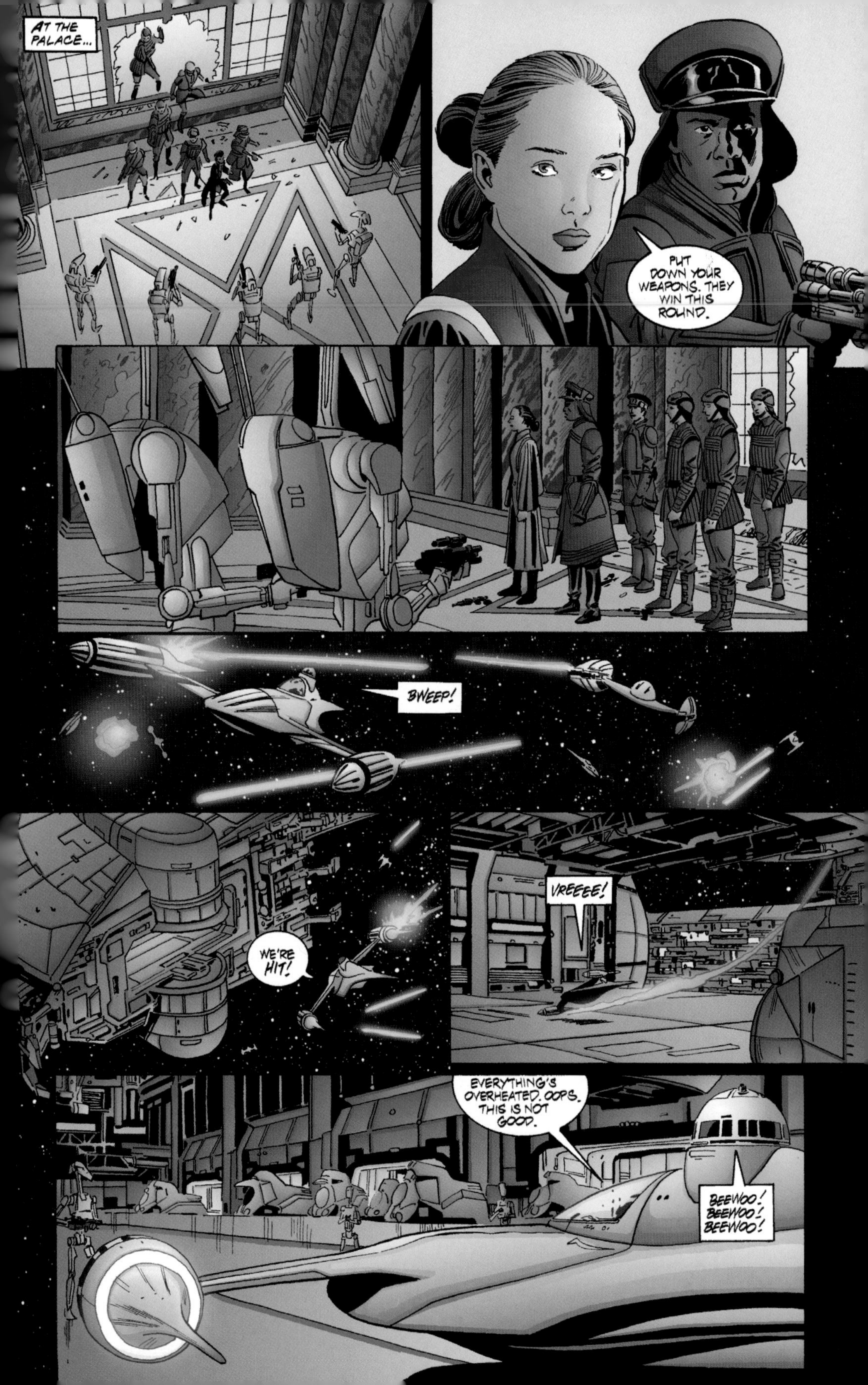
AT THE PALACE...
PUT DOWN YOUR WEAPONS. THEY WIN THIS ROUND.
BWEEP!
WE'RE HIT!
VREEEE!
EVERYTHING'S OVERHEATED. OOPS. THIS IS NOT GOOD.
BEEWOO! BEEWOO! BEEWOO!

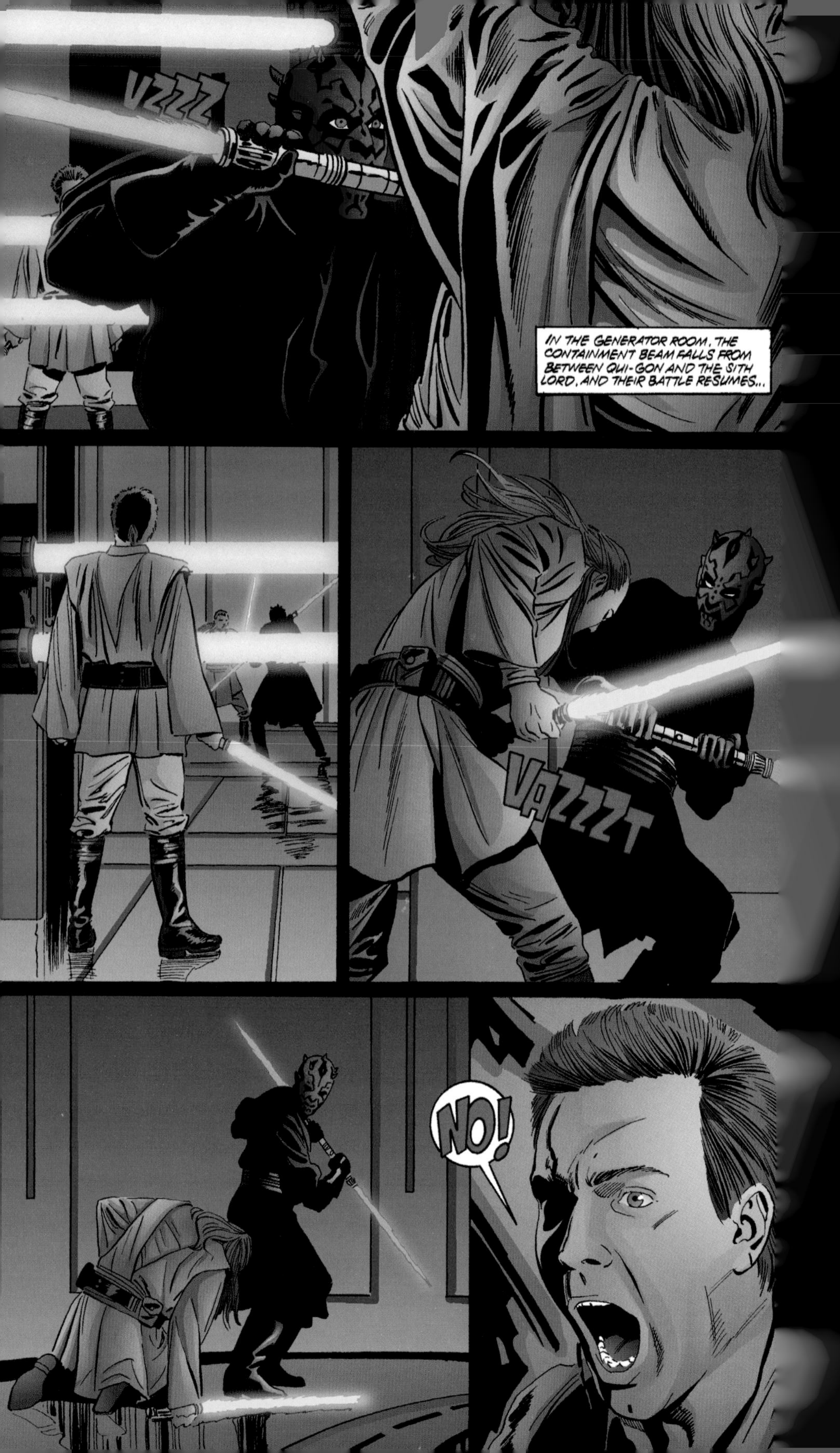
VZZZZ
IN THE GENERATOR ROOM, THE CONTAINMENT BEAM FALLS FROM BETWEEN QUI-GON AND THE SITH LORD, AND THEIR BATTLE RESUMES...
VAZZZZT
NO!

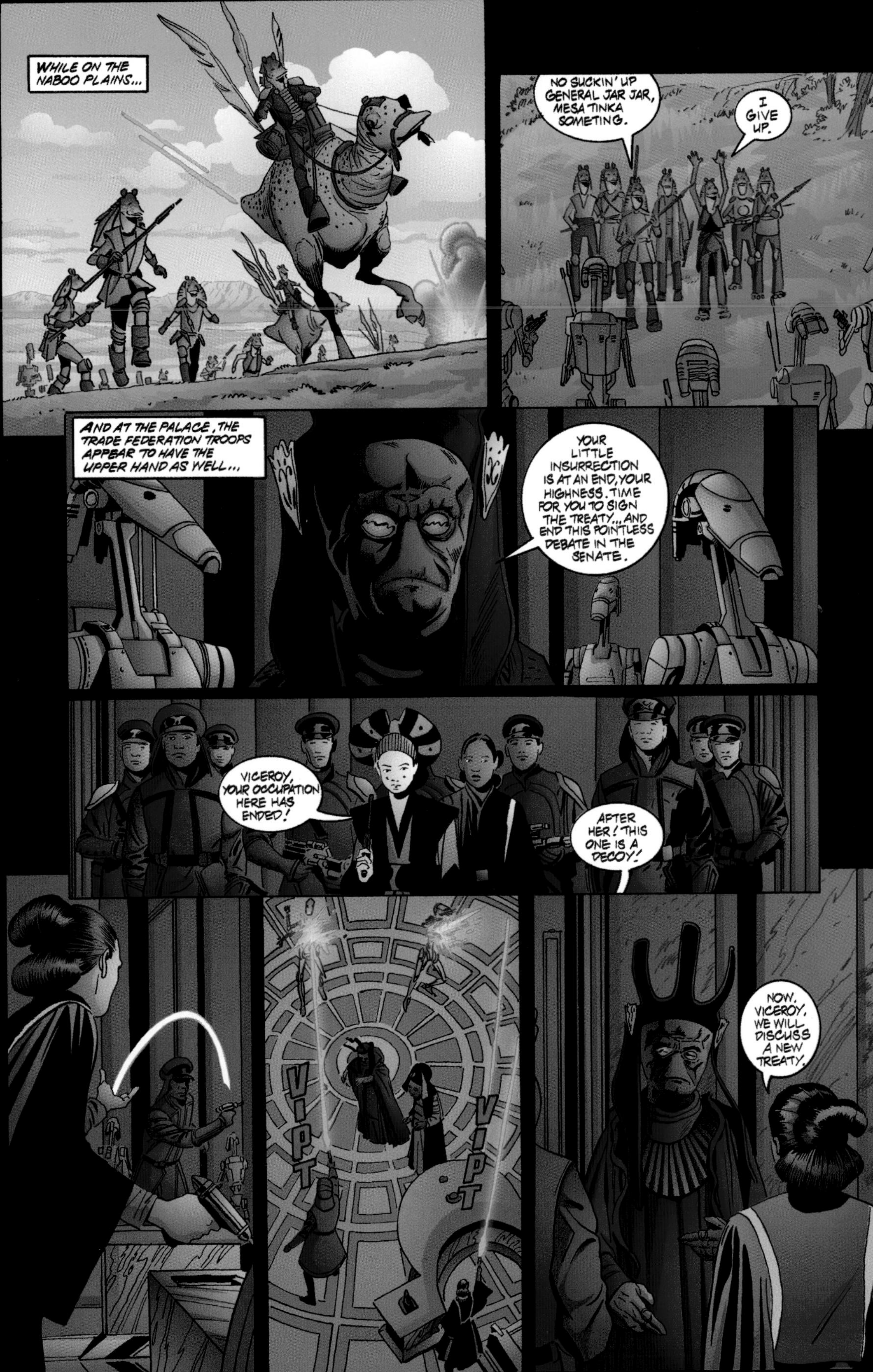
WHILE ON THE NABOO PLAINS...
NO SUCKIN' UP GENERAL JAR JAR, MESA TINKA SOMETING.
I GIVE UP.
AND AT THE PALACE, THE TRADE FEDERATION TROOPS APPEAR TO HAVE THE UPPER HAND AS WELL...
YOUR LITTLE INSURRECTION IS AT AN END, YOUR HIGHNESS. TIME FOR YOU TO SIGN THE TREATY... AND END THIS POINTLESS DEBATE IN THE SENATE.
VICEROY, YOUR OCCUPATION HERE HAS ENDED!
AFTER HER! THIS ONE IS A DECOY!
VIPT
VIPT
NOW, VICEROY, WE WILL DISCUSS A NEW TREATY.

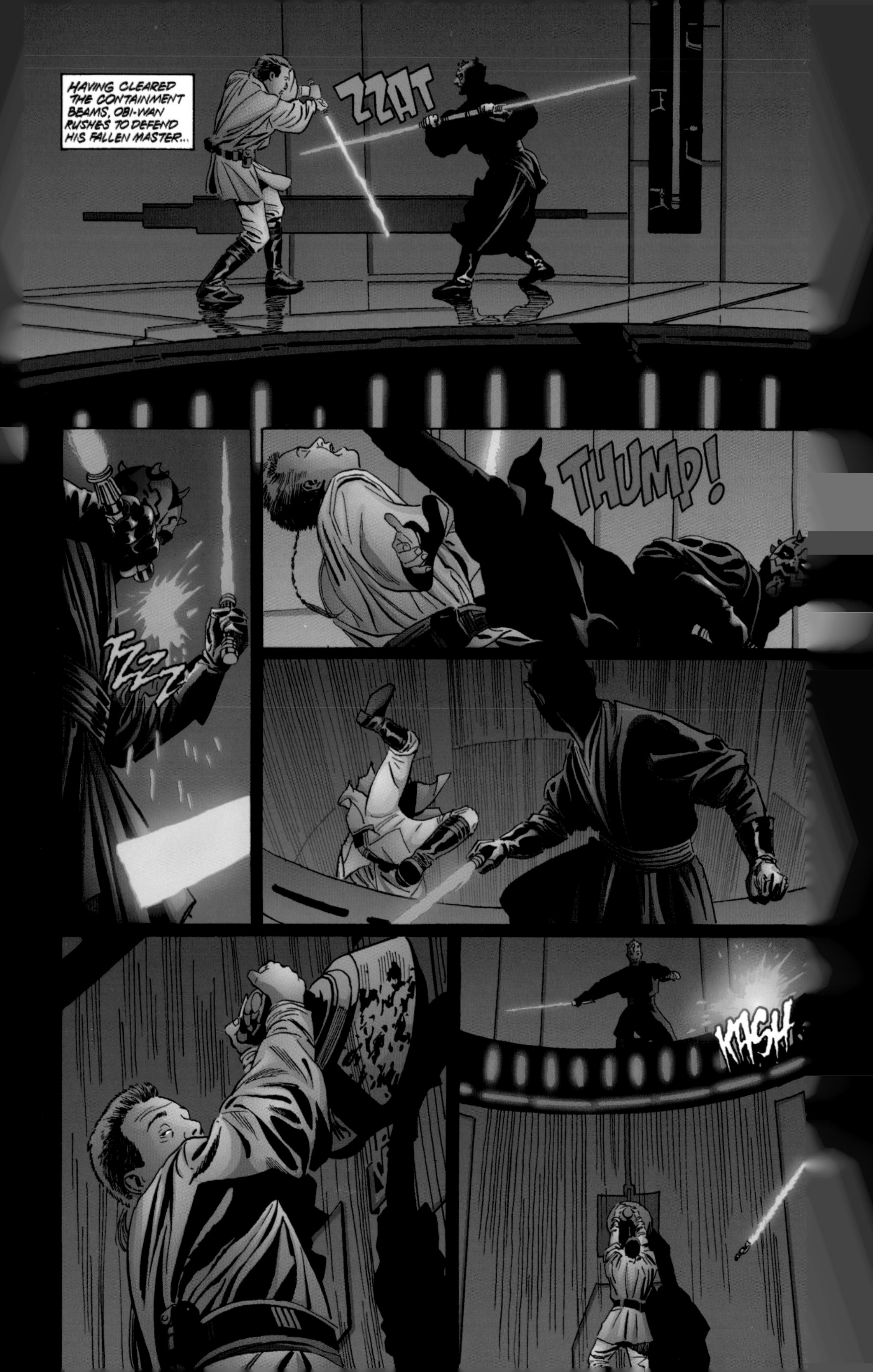
HAVING CLEARED THE CONTAINMENT BEAMS, OBI-WAN RUSHES TO DEFEND HIS FALLEN MASTER...
ZZAT
FZZZ
THUMP!
KASH

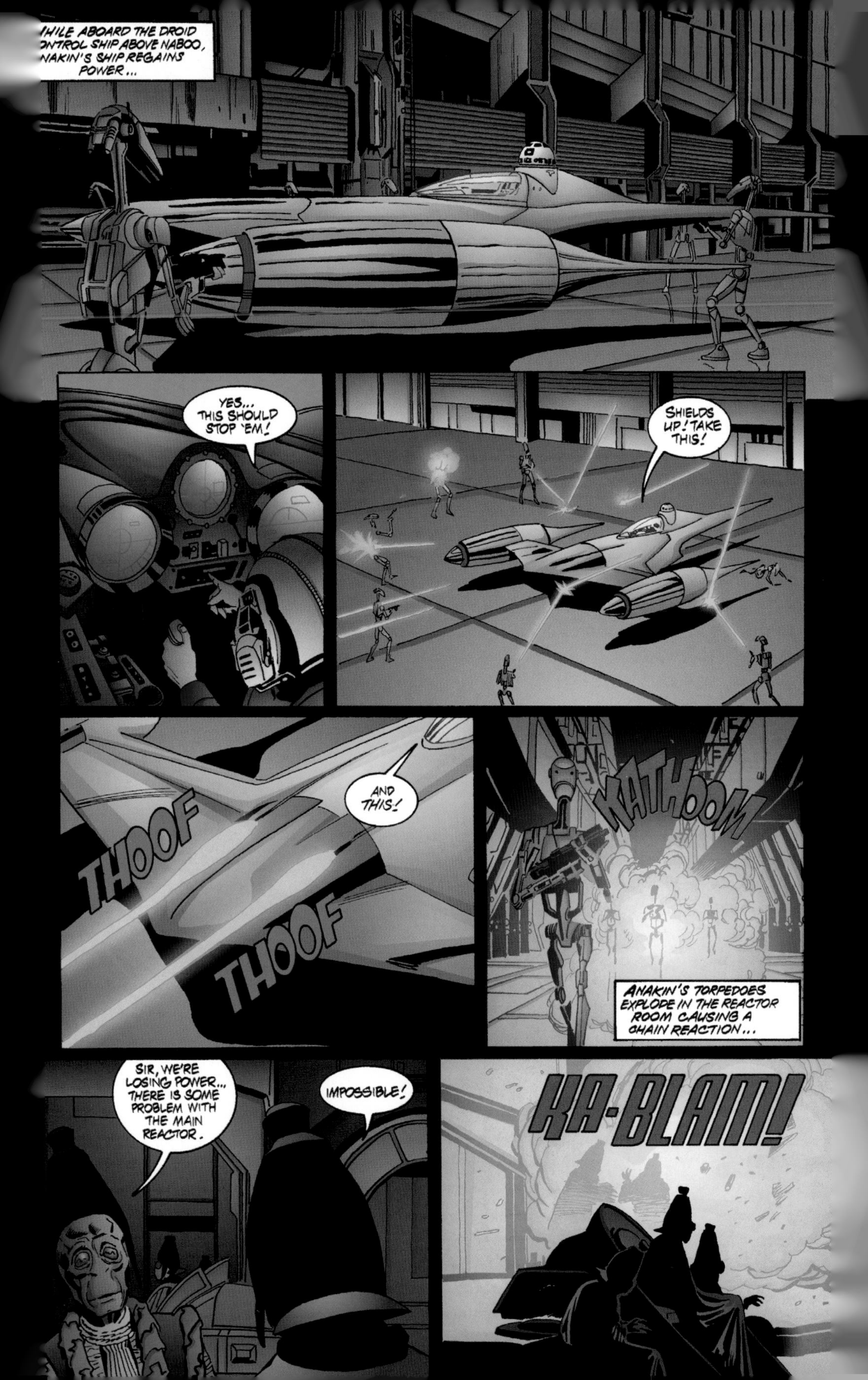

WHILE ABOARD THE DROID CONTROL SHIP ABOVE NABOO, ANAKIN'S SHIP REGAINS POWER...
YES... THIS SHOULD STOP 'EM!
SHIELDS UP! TAKE THIS!
THOOF
AND THIS!
THOOF
KATHOOM
ANAKIN'S TORPEDOES EXPLODE IN THE REACTOR ROOM CAUSING A CHAIN REACTION...
SIR, WE'RE LOSING POWER... THERE IS SOME PROBLEM WITH THE MAIN REACTOR.
IMPOSSIBLE!
KA-BLAM!

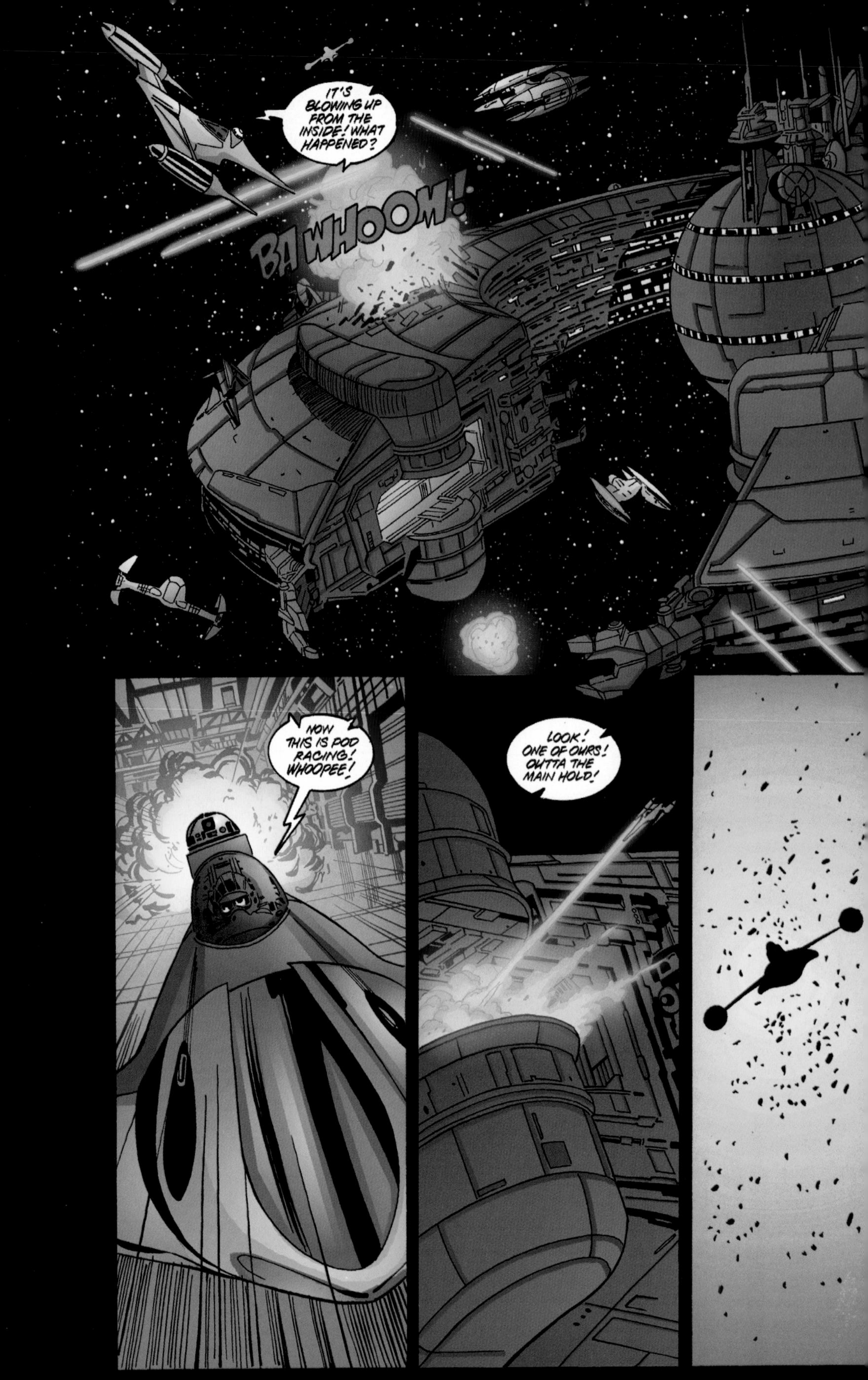
IT'S BLOWING UP FROM THE INSIDE! WHAT HAPPENED?
BA WHOOM!
NOW THIS IS POD RACING! WHOOPEE!
LOOK! ONE OF OURS! OUTTA THE MAIN HOLD!

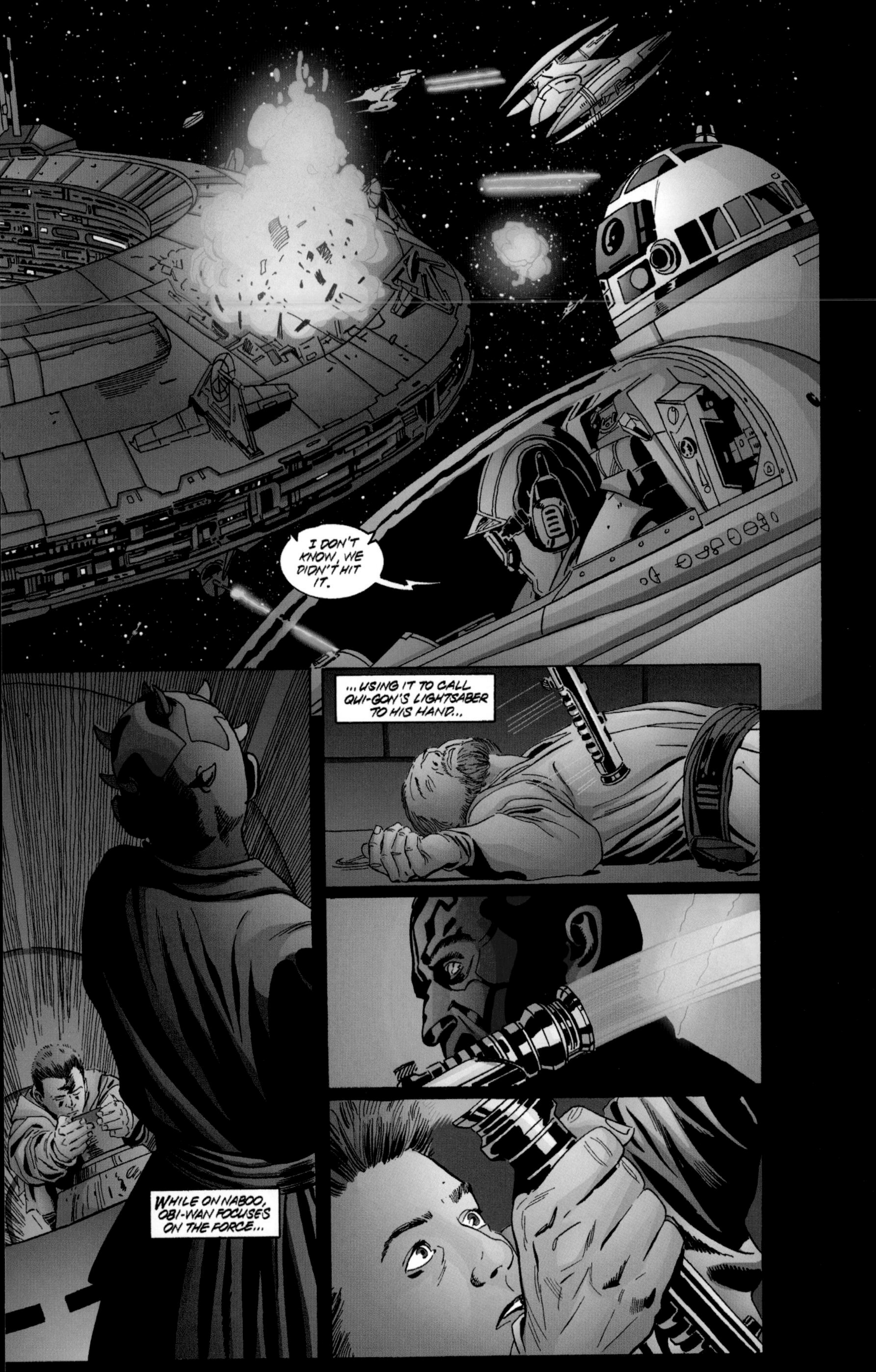
I DON'T KNOW, WE DIDN'T HIT IT.
WHILE ON NABOO, OBI-WAN FOCUSES ON THE FORCE...
...USING IT TO CALL QUI-GON'S LIGHTSABER TO HIS HAND...

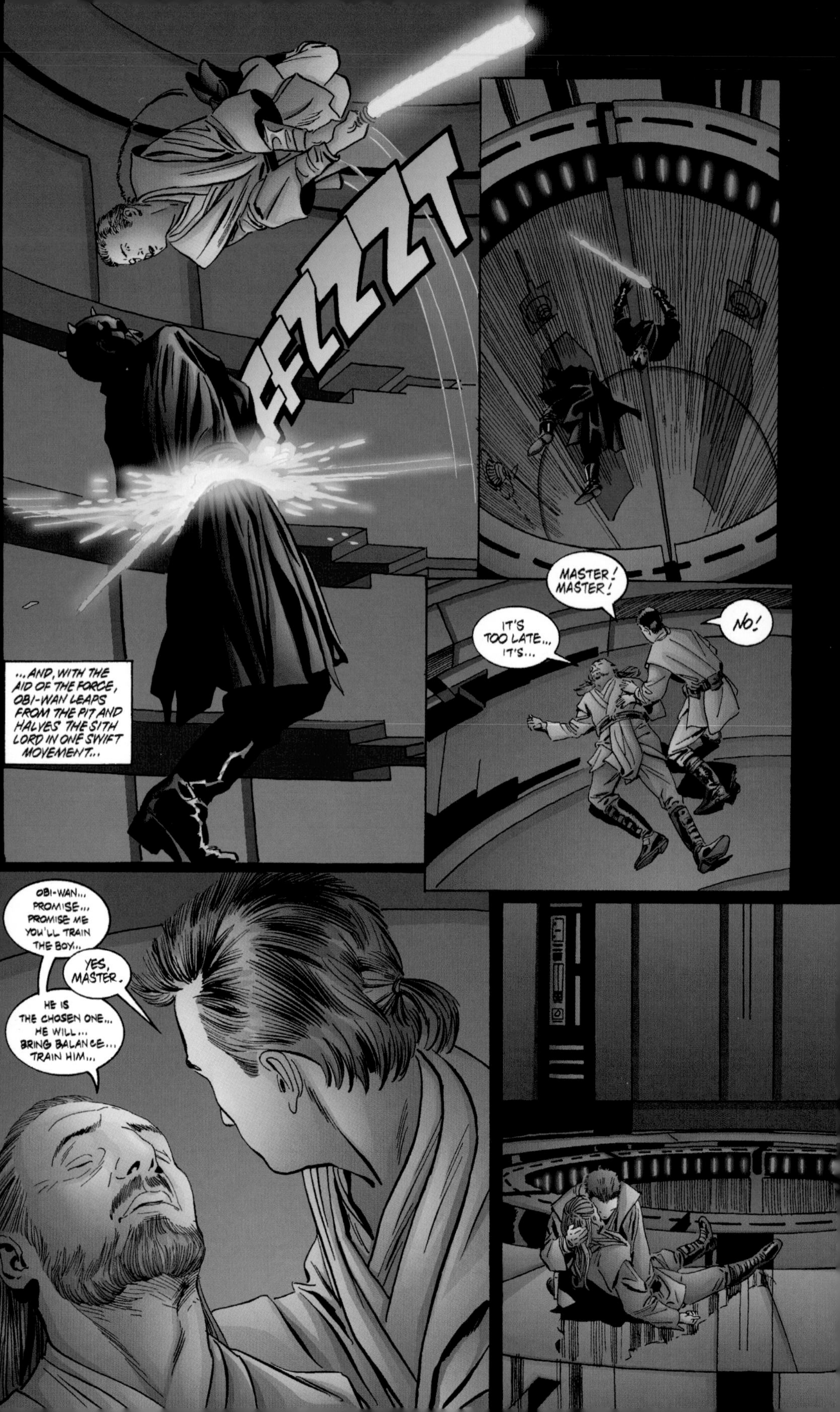
FZZZT
...AND, WITH THE AID OF THE FORCE, OBI-WAN LEAPS FROM THE PIT AND HALVES THE SITH LORD IN ONE SWIFT MOVEMENT...
MASTER! MASTER!
NO!
IT'S TOO LATE... IT'S...
OBI-WAN... PROMISE... PROMISE ME YOU'LL TRAIN THE BOY...
YES, MASTER.
HE IS THE CHOSEN ONE... HE WILL... BRING BALANCE... TRAIN HIM...

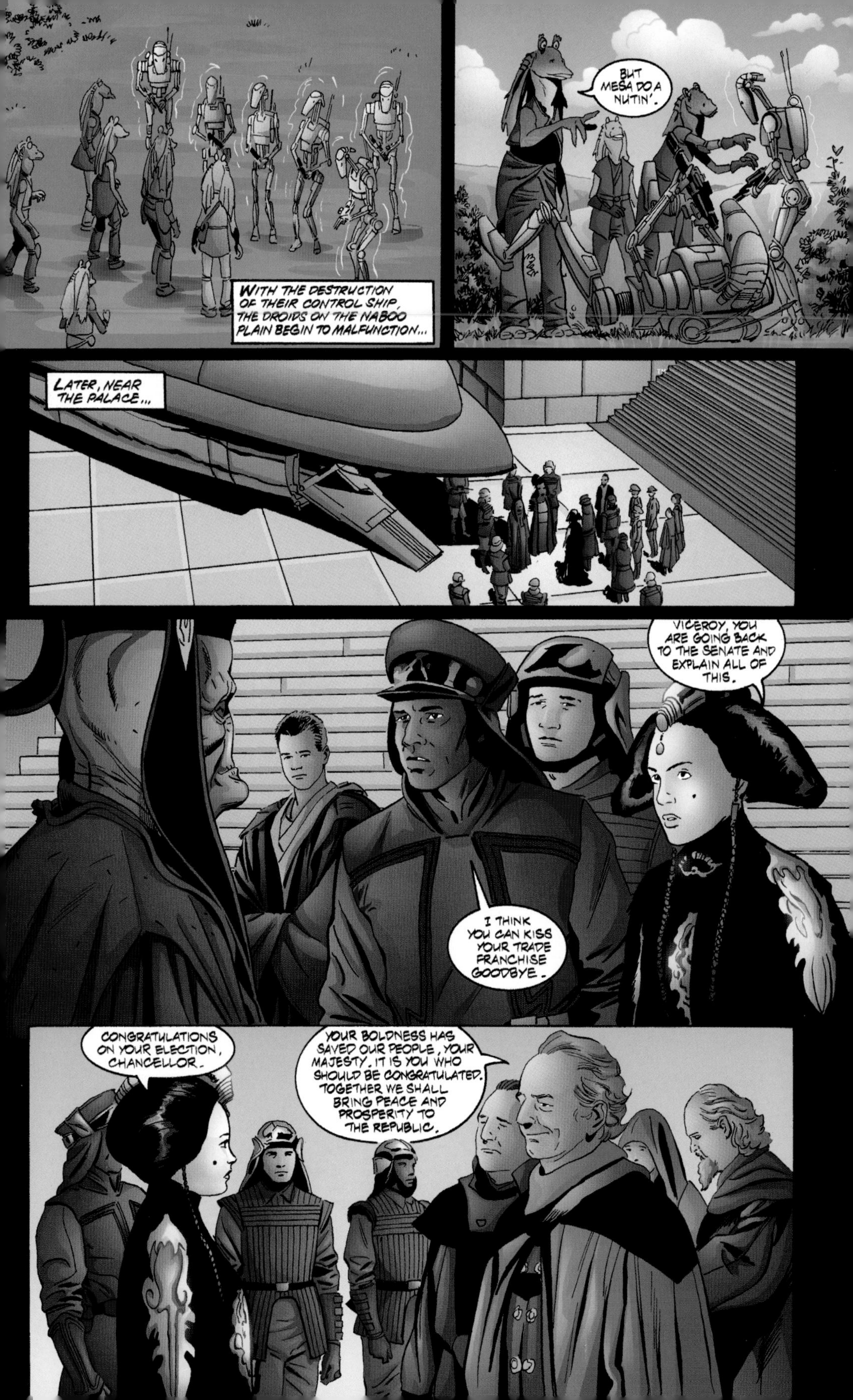
WITH THE DESTRUCTION OF THEIR CONTROL SHIP, THE DROIDS ON THE NABOO PLAIN BEGIN TO MALFUNCTION...
BUT MESA DO A NUTIN'.
LATER, NEAR THE PALACE...
VICEROY, YOU ARE GOING BACK TO THE SENATE AND EXPLAIN ALL OF THIS.
I THINK YOU CAN KISS YOUR TRADE FRANCHISE GOODBYE.
CONGRATULATIONS ON YOUR ELECTION, CHANCELLOR.
YOUR BOLDNESS HAS SAVED OUR PEOPLE, YOUR MAJESTY. IT IS YOU WHO SHOULD BE CONGRATULATED. TOGETHER WE SHALL BRING PEACE AND PROSPERITY TO THE REPUBLIC.

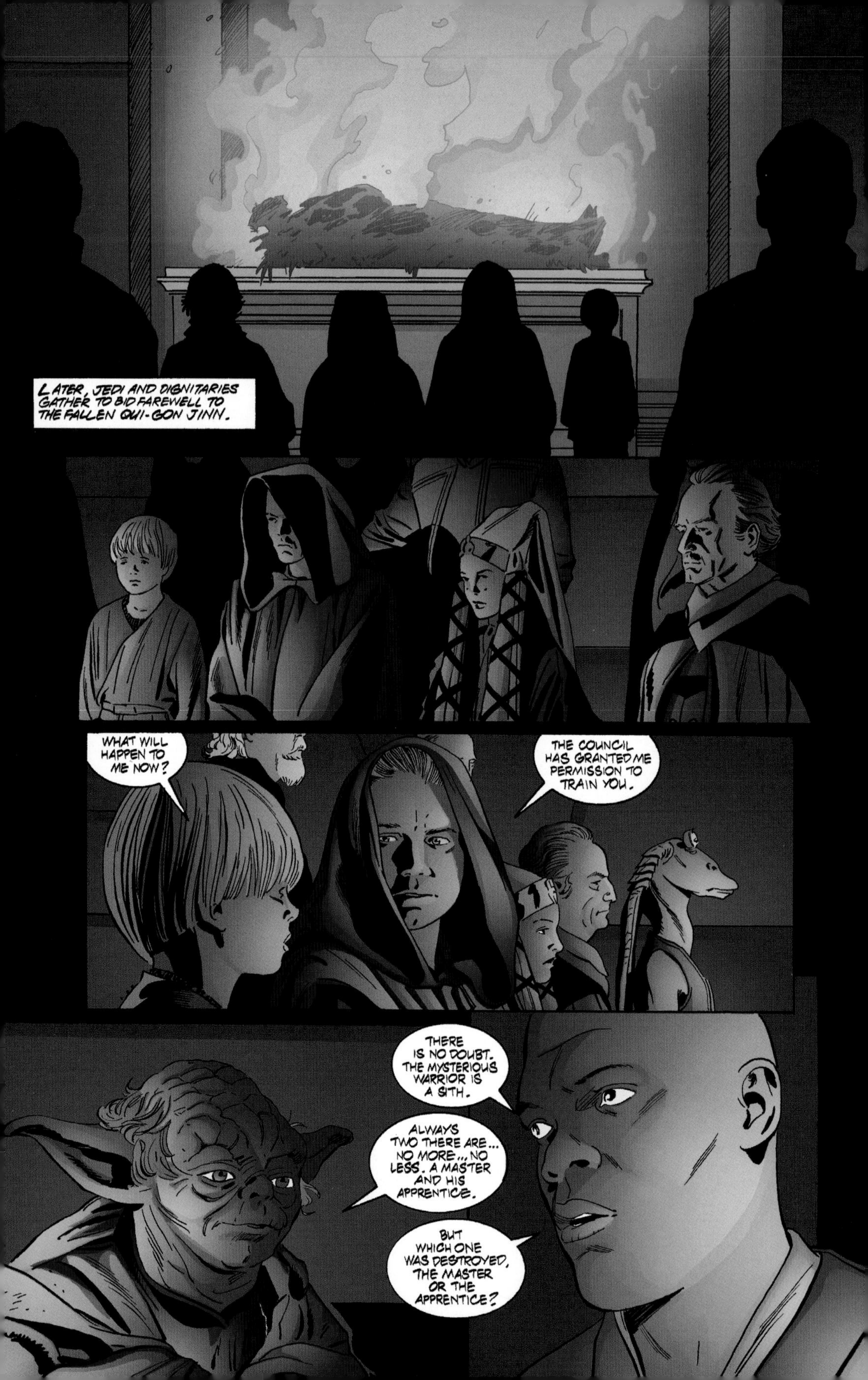
LATER, JEDI AND DIGNITARIES GATHER TO BID FAREWELL TO THE FALLEN QUI-GON JINN.
WHAT WILL HAPPEN TO ME NOW?
THE COUNCIL HAS GRANTED ME PERMISSION TO TRAIN YOU.
THERE IS NO DOUBT. THE MYSTERIOUS WARRIOR IS A SITH.
ALWAYS TWO THERE ARE... NO MORE... NO LESS. A MASTER AND HIS APPRENTICE.
BUT WHICH ONE WAS DESTROYED, THE MASTER OR THE APPRENTICE?

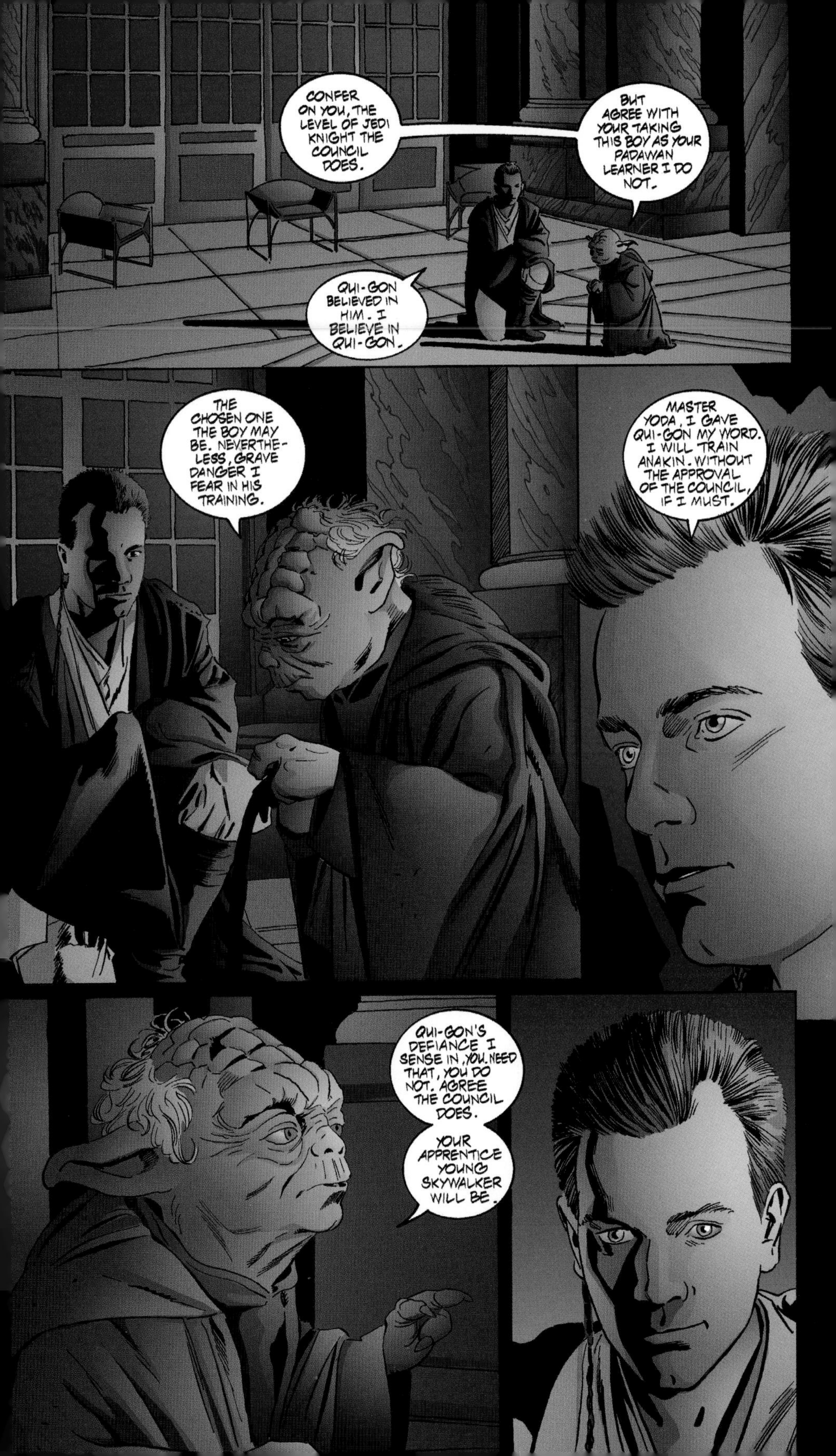
CONFER ON YOU, THE LEVEL OF JEDI KNIGHT THE COUNCIL DOES.
BUT AGREE WITH YOUR TAKING THIS BOY AS YOUR PADAWAN LEARNER I DO NOT.
QUI-GON BELIEVED IN HIM. I BELIEVE IN QUI-GON.
THE CHOSEN ONE THE BOY MAY BE. NEVERTHELESS, GRAVE DANGER I FEAR IN HIS TRAINING.
MASTER YODA, I GAVE QUI-GON MY WORD. I WILL TRAIN ANAKIN. WITHOUT THE APPROVAL OF THE COUNCIL, IF I MUST.
QUI-GON'S DEFIANCE I SENSE IN YOU. NEED THAT, YOU DO NOT. AGREE THE COUNCIL DOES.
YOUR APPRENTICE YOUNG SKYWALKER WILL BE.

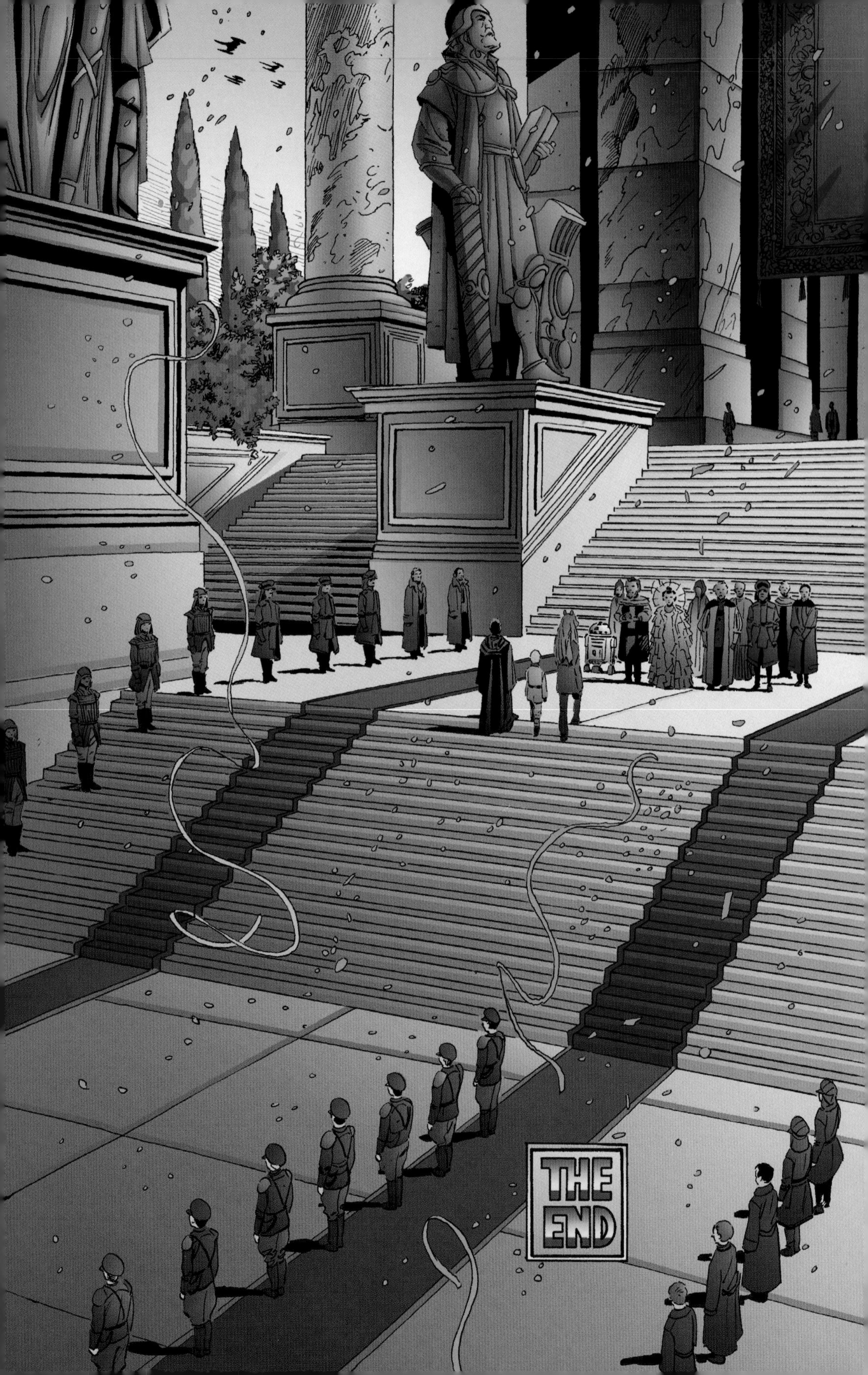
THE END